VOYAGE

POWERLESS NATION: BOOK TWO

ELLISA BARR

For my Mom and my Daughter

CHAPTER ONE

SENA WATCHED SEASONED PASSENGERS jockey for position in the boarding line as though trying to get the best seats at a sold out rock concert -- Neil Diamond or Barry Manilow, judging by their average age.

"Did you remember extra batteries for the camera?" she heard a white-haired woman nag her husband. "You know how they overcharge for everything on the ship."

He patted her shoulder. "Don't worry, dear. Relax and enjoy yourself. I want this to be a trip we never forget."

"I can't relax if we don't actually board," the woman said, glaring pointedly at Sena's school group.

Sena's class was causing a delay for everyone embarking on the cruise ship to Alaska, and her teacher, Ms. Friedel, gestured emphatically to a security officer at the foot of the gangplank. With her strident voice and mop of unruly curls, everyone called her Ms. Frizzle or "The Frizz," behind her back.

Restless students horsed around, a few of the boys shoving each other good-naturedly. Sena noticed a girl point a phone in her direction and snap a photo. Moments later the other girls' phones beeped and they looked at her out of the corners of their eyes and snickered.

The girl who had taken the photo, Charity Van Buren (Charity. Oh, the irony!), had texted her the night before to tell her they were all going to wear their school uniforms at boarding as a show of school spirit.

Sena had made the socially fatal mistake of believing her.

Sena's phone beeped and she reluctantly looked to assess the damage. Sure enough, it was a picture of herself looking lost and out of place. The photo of a small girl stared back at her with long black hair in two braids, and a secondhand uniform that was too big for her. It made her look even younger than her fifteen years. The text read: "Hope the ship has a kiddie club."

Sena sighed and wished the line would start moving. Once the cruise began and there were more interesting diversions, maybe her classmates would leave her alone.

The school cruise was a new idea as an alternative to summer camp. Normally teens wouldn't be allowed to go on a cruise without their parents, but the principal was married to one of the cruise line's board of directors and they'd agreed that with a high enough ratio of teachers to students, they'd give it a try.

Although the cost was exorbitant, for the majority of families with students at the most elite prep school north of Seattle, the price of the ticket didn't merit a second thought. Sena's foster family wasn't well off, but her foster father worked for the school and had pulled some strings to get her the partial scholarship that paid for her ticket.

She'd been thrilled that he'd make such an effort for her until she found out that while she was gone ("out of our hair" were the precise words), her foster parents were taking their *real* kids to Disneyland for a week.

Sena felt a nudge at her shoulder and turned to see Kade McGuire. He was tall and athletic with piercing blue eyes beneath dark brows, and full lips that could curve into the most mesmerizing smile. Sena flushed and Kade pointed ahead of her. The line was moving and she was holding it up.

"Oops, right, sorry," she said, and scurried forward. Why did she always act like a scared rabbit around him?

A crew member asked to see her ID and after glancing at it said, "Welcome aboard, See-nah."

"It's Sena, rhymes with henna," she muttered under her breath as she was handed a bottle of hand sanitizer and a map of the ship.

Once they were finally aboard, the students and chaperones were directed by another crew member to the section of cabins reserved for the school. Before leaving, he announced that everyone had time to stow their carry-ons and then they'd meet for an emergency safety drill at their muster station.

Sena lagged near the back of the group of students. They were assigned four to a room and she decided to let the other girls choose their bunks first and take whatever was left over.

When she reached her assigned room she approached tentatively, not sure of her welcome. The other girls were too busy complaining to notice her.

"Can you believe this place? The closet in my room is bigger than this."

"Do you guys see any outlets besides this one? How are we supposed to charge our phones or do our hair?"

"My mom is going to flip out. They promised her I'd have a window."

Sena glanced inside and for once she agreed with her classmates. The room was miniscule. There were two bunk beds and a tiny bathroom with a single sink and mirror. The closet was more like a cupboard. No tub, no porthole, not even a second bedside table. She slipped inside and climbed to a top bunk.

"I'll sleep up here," she offered down to Charity, "and you can have all of the space under the bed for your luggage."

Charity made a grunting noise that Sena took to mean acceptance, while their roommates bickered over who would get the under bunk space on the other side of the room.

Sena looked around her tiny corner of the ship. There were no cupboards or shelves in which to stash her backpack. The smooth wall was featureless. There wasn't even a place to put her glasses when she went to sleep.

"Did you guys notice if our muster station was on the way in?" Sena asked, looking over the ship map and the evacuation route.

"Mustard station?" asked Jessica, shoving her carry-on under the narrow bed, evidently the winner of the bunk bed argument.

"Muster station. It's where we meet in case of emergency."

Jessica shrugged one spaghetti-strapped shoulder, clearly not interested.

Charity adjusted her make-up in the tiny mirror above the lone bedside table. "What kind of emergency would there be? It's not the Titanic, you know."

Sena tucked the safety card in her backpack. "I'm going to go look around. I'll see you guys at the safety presentation."

"Not if I can help it," said Jessica. "Bo-ring."

"Yeah," agreed Charity, "my folks made me go to one last summer in Europe. You have to put on a life vest some hairy, old guy probably wore on the last cruise."

"Ew," said Paris. "Count me out."

"Hey wait," said Charity, giving Sena her full attention. "You can sign in for us. Please? We'll save you a chair by the pool."

Charity's smile was warm and friendly and for a moment Sena almost believed she actually meant it.

"I guess I could, but you guys should really go. What if there's a test later or something?"

"Whatever," said Charity, turning away to apply lip color. "Just be cool and do it, okay?"

"Okay," Sena agreed in a small voice, closing the door softly behind her.

The ship was pulling out from the dock and Sena found a bench where she could watch the Seattle port slip away. She thought about her foster family, the Clarks. They were probably running around, trying to finish packing for their trip to southern California. Although she'd always wanted to go to Disneyland, Alaska was pretty neat too. At least they hadn't left her with the neighbor and her household of overly-active young children.

A male voice broke into her thoughts. "That's some view, isn't it?" A young man in a crew uniform sat on the bench next to her. "You don't mind do you?"

Sena shook her head and pushed her glasses up.

He went on, "I'm not really supposed to be out here. I'm on duty." He snickered. "I swear, I can't say that with a straight face. Do you know how often they use the word 'duty' on a ship? There's shore duty, on duty, off duty."

"Duty-free," added Sena with a grin, taking an instant

liking to the young man whose nametag said Danny.

His smile matched hers. "That's a good one. Anyway, I'm forsaking my duties so I could catch one last glimpse of Seattle. You won't tell on me, right?"

"Last glimpse? We'll be back in a week."

"You'll be back, but I'm staying in Alaska."

"Wow, really? For good?" Sena thought about what it would be like to leave everything behind and start over from scratch. It sounded like a dream.

"I don't know. Maybe. I'm going to try to get a job working in the fish hatcheries for the rest of the summer. I might stick around if I like it."

He scanned the area and then glanced back at Sena. "I haven't told my boss I'm jumping ship. I doubt he'll be surprised though. They keep telling me I won't last the trip because I'm a spoiled American. Have you noticed that most of the crew is made up of foreigners?"

Sena shook her head.

"It's true. They work for a lot less than we do and they work way harder. You wouldn't believe the hours they put me down for. Two weeks straight without a day off and only six hours or so to sleep. They're crazy."

"They say you have to be crazy to work in a fish hatchery too." Her comment surprised both of them and she blushed.

The sailor laughed. "You got me there." Then he jumped to his feet as another member of the crew approached.

"Danny wasn't bothering you was he, Miss?"

"Oh no, not at all," said Sena, thinking quickly. "Actually, I was feeling a little seasick and he helped me find a place to sit down and offered to stay with me until I felt better."

"Is that so?" The older crewman looked from Sena to Danny. Danny had been waggling his eyebrows at her over the crewman's shoulder and froze mid-waggle.

"I'm feeling a bit better now," said Sena, getting to her feet, trying not to smile.

"And I've got duties to attend to," said Danny with a merry look.

Sena choked back her laughter.

"Maybe I'll see you around," he said, turning to wave as he walked away down the hallway.

Sena waved back, not able to think of a reply until after he'd turned a corner and was out of sight.

Fifteen minutes later a voice over the ship's PA system announced that it was time for the mandatory safety presentation. Sena looked around when she got to the muster station and wasn't surprised that her bunkmates weren't there.

The meeting reminded her of the seatbelt tutorial given at the beginning of flights, only this one focused on life jackets and lifeboats. Afterwards, everyone in attendance had to check in with the key cards to their rooms, and Sena ran into trouble.

The staff person in charge of the roll was keeping a close eye on it, making sure procedure was followed. "I'm sorry, Miss, you can only check in for yourself."

"My friends were here until now, but they had to leave before they could show you their cards." Even though Sena hated lying for Charity and her friends, she didn't want to make any problems for them either.

"Well," said the staff person with forced cheerfulness, "they can check in when they get back or we'll send someone down to their room to find them."

Sena left, feeling unhappy that not only had she lied, it had been pointless anyway. She knew she should have stood up to Charity in the first place and told her she wouldn't do it, but Sena avoided conflict whenever she could. Although she didn't care if Charity liked her, she didn't want to make her mad.

Sena decided to eat dinner on the Lido deck. There was an open buffet and the amount and variety of the food was nearly overwhelming.

As she approached the buffet table, she had a flashback to another buffet: a hotel breakfast buffet when she was eleven years old.

She had sneaked in the side door of the hotel when a guest exited, and followed her nose to the breakfast lounge. In front of her was a hungry child's dream, but she didn't pause to admire. This wasn't the first time Sena had scavenged a meal from a hotel buffet and she knew what she wanted. She piled a plate with fruit, bread, packets of peanut butter and jelly, and a couple of containers of yogurt. Pretty much anything she thought would survive being in her pockets all day. She also took a packaged blueberry muffin for her mom. Those were her favorite.

When she turned away from the buffet she felt a hand on her arm. "Not so fast, missy. I'm going to need to see your room card."

Sena looked up and saw a big man wearing a name tag that read: Mark - Hotel Security.

She was in big trouble.

"Sure," she said, trying for cool despite the squeak in her voice. She didn't know what they did to thieves. If they put her in jail she didn't think anyone would come get her out.

Sena went through the motions of checking her pockets for the nonexistent key card while the guard watched with obvious impatience. Other people in the breakfast lounge were taking notice and her heart began to flutter in her chest like a scared bird.

"I guess you're going to tell me it's back in your room?"

Sena nodded, not looking at the security guard.

"Which room would that be?"

Her voice came out in a whisper, "I don't remember."

"Listen, kid, I don't want to see you in here again, and I'm giving your description to the other hotels in the area. Eat breakfast on someone else's dime."

He held out a hand for her plate. Sena looked longingly at her food, and then placed the plate into the guard's hand with shaking fingers.

A touch on her arm snapped her back to the present and Sena gave a surprised yelp. She'd been so caught up in the memory she hadn't noticed what was going on around her. Kade stood looking at her with a bemused smile on his face. "Holding up the line again, Sena?"

Sena was so unsettled by the unhappy memory and disconcerted by the fact he knew her name that she was at a complete loss for words.

Kade shook his head and stepped around her. Sena followed along at his elbow, struggling to find her voice. Kade piled the food so high on his plate she was afraid the whole thing would topple over. She didn't know what half of it was.

"Do you like the cruise so far?" Sena wished she could take the words back as soon as they were out of her mouth. What a stupid question. She sounded like a nine-year-old.

"Sure," Kade replied easily. "What's not to like? I can't wait to see some icebergs. How cool will that be? Soaking in a hot tub and seeing icebergs float by."

A female voice called Kade's name and he turned to look at a table where some of the other kids from their high school were sitting.

"Kade, come on, we're saving you a seat."

"Hey listen, I've gotta run," he said to Sena. "I'll see you around."

She sat apart from the other kids at dinner, listening to their laughter and wishing she knew how to fit in. Whenever she tried, something from her past slipped out and things got awkward. As much as she wanted to have some friends, or even *one* friend, it was too complicated. It was easier to follow the rules, do what people said, and try not to draw too much attention to herself.

After dinner, she checked in with Ms. Friedel well before curfew and then went to her cabin for the night. She rolled her eyes when she discovered the cruise staff had delivered three large suitcases. She wondered why her roommates needed so many suitcases when their clothing was all so skimpy.

She changed quickly into pajamas and then turned on a small book light before climbing the ladder to her bed. From a pocket of her backpack, she pulled a creased and much-read letter from its envelope and read it to herself. Though she'd memorized it, she still liked to see the ink on the page and think of her mother taking the time to write to her.

The bed was soft, the small pool of yellow light was

comforting in the dark room, and it wasn't long before her eyes closed and the letter came to rest gently on her chest.

Sena fell into a sleep so deep she didn't hear the laughter of her roommates when they came in much later than curfew, or their cursing as they tripped and struggled to maneuver around their mountain of luggage.

CHAPTER TWO

THE NEXT MORNING SENA joined some of her classmates for a special tour of the ship. Their guide was an energetic young woman neatly dressed in a jacket and slim fitting skirt with a scarf tied at a cheerful angle. She said her name was Lydia, and, hearing her accent, Sena guessed she was from England.

The tour started in a large theater where the group was escorted backstage to meet some of the cast and production staff. They were preparing for a sold-out performance that night, and Sena was amazed by how friendly and calm they all were.

Sena noticed one actress in particular — the star of the show. She was very beautiful and the other actors treated her almost like their queen bee. She introduced herself as Mona, before smiling graciously at the students and excusing herself.

Next they went down to the galley, which Sena learned was the nautical word for kitchen. Florescent lights reflected from shiny stainless steel metal surfaces everywhere. Even the ceiling and walls were stainless steel.

Workers dressed all in white with tall hats and pristine aprons scurried around preparing the day's meals. Sena was fascinated by the efficiency of their movements while they laid out plates for over six hundred salads and assembled them with astonishing speed and beauty.

The ship also had its own bakery where all of the day's bread, rolls and cookies were baked each morning. The rich, dense smell of fresh baked bread was tantalizing, and Sena's mouth began to water.

"Wouldn't it be easier to buy the bread already made?" one of the students asked.

"It would," said Lydia, "but space is a major concern on a cruise ship, and baked goods take up a lot of room. Besides," she said with a smile as she passed out warm scones to the group, "isn't this better than Wonder Bread?"

While they ate their scones, the guide walked them through the grill area and pointed out that the ship galleys had everything that a traditional hotel or restaurant kitchen had except for one thing. She looked to see if anyone knew what it was. "I'll give out a free soda voucher to anyone that can tell me what's missing."

Sena studied the room. One chef cooked rows and rows of hamburgers on a giant griddle while another stood on a stool to stir a tub of pulled pork with a spatula so big it could be used to row a boat.

"I'll give you a clue," said Lydia. "Look at how he's cooking the burgers."

One of the boys shouted out, "No fire! He's grilling without fire."

"Exactly. Fire is the biggest danger to a ship, so no open flames are allowed in cruise kitchens."

"How do you explain my crème brûlée last night?" asked a female student.

"Aren't you smart?" said Lydia, amused. "While we do have an exception for crème brûlée torches, those must be used in a specific part of the galley, next to the fire extinguisher. Who can guess how much food the kitchens will prepare in a typical week's cruise?"

There were a few wrong guesses before Lydia said, "On this trip we will go through six tons of beef, chicken and seafood."

"So is that, like, two tons of each of those?"

"No, it's like six tons of each of those." Lydia was rewarded by the group's collective sound of amazement.

"Not only that, we'll use over seventy thousand eggs and more than three thousand gallons of soda pop on this trip. Now, does anyone want to see where we keep it all?"

They all did, so they headed to another deck where most of the food was stored. A long hallway with a bumpy rubber floor going the length of the ship stretched out in front of them, with stainless steel doors on both sides.

"We have over thirty different refrigerator and freezer units down here, and a few on other floors as well," she said as she opened door after door to let them see inside.

A massive freezer room held frozen fish and meat at one temperature, and another kept ice cream at a different temperature. One entire walk-in refrigerator room stored the produce for salads, while another held fruit and yet another was full of sides of beef and fresh, whole chickens. The ship even had its own butchers.

"How do they keep track of so much food?" asked one of the teachers. "I hardly remember what I've got in my fridge at home."

"I'm glad you asked. We have a high-tech meal count system that uses a scanner to log every plate prepared in each of the ship's eight kitchens. A computer screen in the main galley shows our executive chef exactly what's being served, so he can precisely control the menu."

As they began to walk out of the seafood freezer, Sena caught a glimpse of a room that looked surprisingly similar to morgues she'd seen on TV shows.

"Excuse me," she asked the guide timidly, "what's stored in there?"

"Funny you should notice that," said Lydia. "It's not part of the tour, but since you asked I supposed I can mention it. Have you ever thought about what happens if someone dies in the middle of a cruise?"

Sena's classmates began pushing to get a glimpse at the room, peppering the guide with questions.

"Are there any bodies in there right now?"

"How many people have died so far this year?"

"Has anyone ever been murdered on your ship?"

The tour guide held her hands up to try to stem the tide of questions. "No, there aren't any bodies in there right now, and no, no one has ever been murdered onboard the *Duchess*. You may have noticed there's a higher ratio of elderly people on the cruise, and it's inevitable that now and then someone will pass away of natural causes. All cruise ships are required to have their own morgue. Ours is refrigerated."

Lydia held up her hands to discourage any more questions about the morgue and said, "Let's go see the engine room."

The engine room reminded Sena of a war room in a military movie. Every wall was covered with computer screens. Some showed camera feeds from different parts of the actual engine area, while others tracked and displayed an unending flow of information about the ship's operations. There were several panels of buttons and switches and a large table covered in Plexiglas that showed detailed diagrams of every level of the ship.

"Brilliant!" Lydia said. "Our Chief Technical Officer, Chief Huang is here this morning."

A man in a white jumpsuit rose to his feet and smiled at them. He had intelligent, brown eyes.

"Welcome to my world," he said, gesturing at the room. "This is where we generate the power for pretty much everything that happens on the ship. Think of it as the heart of the ship. In here is where my technical team monitors every detail of the ship's operations, from the speed of the propellers right down to the water supply in each of your cabins.

"Running a ship takes an unbelievable amount of energy and we generate almost all of it right here. The electricity we generate powers the mechanical system to propel the boat and the water desalinization system which provides most of our drinking water. We use electricity to maintain water pressure, lights, and satellite TV signals to all of the cabins, and we power the food storage and preparation areas you just saw."

"What happens if there's a power outage?" asked one of the girls.

"Since we generate our own power, electrical outages are pretty rare," Chief Huang answered. "The biggest risk to our power comes from an engine overheating, which can cause fires." He indicated several of the screens with video feeds. "See this right here? This is one of the engines. Notice how no one is in the room? That's because it's over 140 degrees Fahrenheit in there."

"So what if there *was* a fire?" asked Sena, realizing he hadn't really answered the question. "What happens if the ship loses power?"

"In the unlikely event that the ship loses power, we

have backup generators next to the main generators, and they would kick in. They wouldn't produce enough electricity for the whole ship, but we could keep critical systems online, like water pressure, lights, and power to the kitchens."

"Would we still be able to move?"

"Yes, in all but the worst case scenario. Now," he said, abruptly changing the subject. "Who wants to meet the captain? Your final stop is the bridge."

The bridge was on a much higher deck. When they walked in, Sena saw four people. The captain was a pale, middle-aged man who looked up in surprise when they entered. Next to him sat Mona, the lead actress Sena recognized from earlier in the theater. He whispered something to her that made her giggle and they both rose to their feet.

"Welcome to the bridge of the *Duchess*, kids. Sorry I can't show you around, but my crew knows the ropes." He turned to one of the other two crewmen and said, "Staff Captain Brady, you have the bridge."

"Aye, aye, Sir," responded one of the crewmen. He stood up as the captain took the actress by the hand and led her off the bridge. Sena searched the faces of the others in the room; if this behavior was unusual, she couldn't tell by their expressions.

The view from the bridge was so amazing, she soon forgot all about the captain. The room had floor to ceiling windows on every side, allowing for an unobstructed view of the sea all around them.

Computer screens and equipment displayed information about the weather forecast, the number of passengers aboard, the location of the ship and much more. Front and center was an oversized office type chair which she assumed was the captain's chair, and on one side of the room was an old fashioned ship's wheel.

Lydia offered to let the kids take photos and they jumped at the chance, sitting in the captain's chair and pretending to steer the ship with the large wheel.

Sena was waiting for a turn at the wheel when she was distracted by an urgent need to know where the nearest restroom was. Glancing around, she had a moment of anxiety until she saw a few steps leading down to a hallway, and a small sign with the familiar symbol for bathroom.

Sena looked for Lydia so she could tell her where she was going, but the guide was on the ship's phone talking to a member of her staff about their next tour that afternoon. Sena didn't want to interrupt, so she slipped into the bathroom, sure she'd be back before anyone noticed she was missing.

If the ship's bridge was high-tech, the bathroom was as basic as it got. She sat down and got out her phone to look through photos of the tour. Flipping further back, she caught sight of a picture of her foster family. It was a candid shot she'd taken while they were at a friend's barbecue.

Her foster parents were sitting together on a porch swing, holding their two young children on their laps and laughing at something. She stared at the photo for a while and wondered where they were and whether they missed her at all.

Without warning, the screen of her phone flickered and turned off. A moment later, the bathroom light went out too, leaving Sena in total darkness. A wave of panic washed over her. Bad things had happened to her in the dark, and now she avoided it at all costs.

She waved her hand in the air, thinking maybe the light was motion activated, but it remained off.

With shaking hands she fumbled to turn her phone back on. All she needed was a glimmer of light, enough to stop the darkness from pressing in on her skin and her eyes. She felt like it was choking her. Why wouldn't her phone turn on?

Sena cursed under her breath. She'd probably used up the battery taking photos on the tour.

It's just a bathroom, she told herself firmly, trying to slow her breathing. Her legs were so weak with fear that they wobbled under her when she finally managed to stand up.

In slow motion, she felt her way around the small bathroom until she found the light switch. She flicked it off and on. Nothing happened. No matter, she'd found the door.

Sena tried to recover her composure before going out. She wiped her tears away and reached for the handle.

She wasn't prepared at all for what she saw when she opened the door.

All the flat screen TVs on the walls of the bridge were off, as was the radar monitor, and Sena thought perhaps they were staging some kind of drill for the benefit of the kids. On the other side of the room, Lydia hustled the last of the students off the bridge.

The staff captain barked orders at the other crewman and Sena was paralyzed at the thought of crossing the room to the exit and possibly getting yelled at. She shrank back against the bathroom door. There weren't any lights in the small hallway and she was partially hidden in shadows. She'd stay here until things calmed down or she saw an opportunity to sneak away.

Though all the lights in the room were off, sunlight flooded in through the windows and she had a good view of what was going on. The staff captain picked up the bridge phone. "Chief Huang, are you there? Adam, can you hear me?" He held the phone to his ear for a moment and then turned to the other crewman in the room. "Go get the captain. Tell him we've got no power and no communications on the bridge."

"Yes, sir," the other man responded and quickly left the room.

The staff captain picked up the intercom, which didn't seem to be working either. Sena heard him mumble to himself and saw him fiddle with the controls. Then something caught his eye and he gasped. Sena took a step forward to see what he was looking at.

She couldn't be seeing it right. Sena pushed her glasses up higher on her nose.

There was no mistaking it now.

They stood in horror as a passenger airplane crashed into the ocean no more than half a mile from the ship and burst into flames.

CHAPTER THREE

SENA HEARD SCREAMS AND thought for a brief moment they came from the plane, before she realized passengers on the decks above the bridge had also seen the crash. Their cries of horror filled the air as they witnessed the tragedy unfolding directly before the ship.

If they were to avoid sailing through the disaster, the staff captain would have to change course, and with that thought, Sena realized the ever present sound of the engines was no longer in the background. The ship wasn't moving. Not only that, it was slowly listing to one side. Pencils and other round objects rolled off tables and onto the floor.

The staff captain touched his fingers to forehead and chest in a religious gesture and then tried the ship's radio. "Mayday! Mayday! This is Staff Captain Brady of the *Duchess*. There's a large passenger plane down at location 53, 53.4 North, 169, 584 West. Requesting immediate rescue support."

No response from the radio.

The sound of running footsteps in the hall signaled Sena to press back into the shadows. The door burst open and Captain Crane rushed in, followed by Mona and several other crewmen.

"Status report," barked the captain.

"Sir, we've lost all power and comms to the bridge.

Power to the ship appears to be down but there's no report yet from the engine room. Radio is down, radar is down. And there's…" He trailed off, pointing to the wreckage of the airplane, where flames appeared to float on the water. "What are your orders?"

The captain stared at the burning plane, lost in thought. The actress nudged him and his attention shifted back. He snapped at one of his crew, "Get down to the engine room and find out what's going on. I want the power back on now." The crewman left the room at a run and the captain pointed at another. "Find Lydia and send her in. Why isn't she here already?"

Another sailor raced away.

"What's wrong with you people? Why are you all standing there? We have to keep the passengers calm." He moaned and sank into the captain's chair. "I do not need this. Do you know how much bad press we'll get for losing power? I'll be ruined."

"Sir," said the staff captain, "what about the plane?"

"What *about* the plane?"

"We need to go out and check the wreckage. There could have been survivors."

"Don't tell me what I need to do, Brady. Look at that mess! There's no way anyone survived that. If they didn't die on impact they're rotisserie chicken by now. We've got our own problems to deal with."

Sena couldn't believe what she was hearing. From the look on the staff captain's face, and several others in the room, she wasn't the only one.

"But, sir, we could just—"

"I said no. If this is a terrorist attack I need my people here, ready for action."

"Terrorists?" gasped the actress, collapsing

dramatically in a nearby chair.

The captain's tone changed. "Don't worry, my dear. You'll be safe with me." He gave her a comforting look and then turned on the crew again, "Where's my security chief? And where's the IT guy? Why don't we have back-up power yet?" He raised his voice, "And why is everyone still sitting around? I want answers. Now!"

Sena decided it was time to get out of there. Before she could go, a member of the crew burst onto the bridge.

"Fire in the engine room!" he shouted.

"Get a hold of yourself, man," said the captain. "What's the situation down there?"

The man spoke in quick bursts between ragged breaths. "They don't know how it started. The monitors and lights went dead at the same time, so Chief Huang sent someone to check on the engines. Number four engine is an inferno, and we don't have any fire suppression or water pressure. Back-up generators are down."

"Fire doors?"

"Will have to be closed manually, sir."

"I see," said the captain, turning again to gaze out the full-length windows at the flaming wreckage of the airplane. He was silent a long moment, lost in thought. It was an awkward silence that should have been filled with emergency orders and ship-wide reports.

When the captain faced his crew again he said, "Brady, you were right about that airplane. I'll take a lifeboat over there myself. Anyone who wants to join me —we are going now."

"But sir," began Brady, "you can't leave now."

Captain Crane ignored him and helped the actress to

her feet. "Come, my love, let's get you off this ship."

Brady blocked the doorway. "I insist, Captain. You can't abandon ship. She needs her captain."

Tension in the room was high, and for a moment Sena thought the captain might strike his officer. Instead, he pushed him aside and headed for the door. "Staff Captain Brady, you have the bridge."

With that, the captain led the majority of the ship's commanding officers out of the room.

Staff Captain Brady looked at the remaining crewmen and took a deep breath. "Thank you for your sacrifice. Daryl, grab a bullhorn and get passengers to their muster stations. Same for you Oscar. Passengers are our first priority."

"Yes, Captain!" Daryl and Oscar left at a run.

Sena noticed they hadn't called him 'Staff Captain.'

The captain spoke to the remaining man, "Ryan, I need you to alert the fire patrol. I'm hoping they are already activated, but without comms there's no way to be sure. Then I need you to get the fire doors closed."

The man took a step back. "All of them?"

"Do your best. You're dismissed."

When the man left the bridge, Sena gathered her courage and stepped out of the shadows. "I'd like to help if I can." Even though she'd intended to sound convincing, her voice came out unsteady.

Captain Brady looked surprised. "How did you get in here? You need to get to your muster station right now. That's an order."

"I saw—"

"Never mind any of that. The only thing that matters now is getting everyone ready to evacuate. That includes you."

Sena looked into the man's face. He was slim and young, but steady, and there was resolve in his eyes.

"Yes sir," she said. As she left, the room flooded with more members of the ship's crew, all clamoring to help. She had to admire how quickly the staff captain had stepped into his new role. She knew how hard it was when people you counted on let you down.

Captain Brady had the heart of a true captain. Maybe they'd survive this after all.

When Sena stepped out from the staff-only door, she immediately noticed the smell of burning plastic and hot metal. There were people all around her and she was soon swept along in the crush of panicked passengers trying to get to the lifeboats. After getting her bearings and making sure they were taking her in the right direction, Sena allowed herself to be carried along with the crowd.

Many of the passengers were in swimsuits, probably coming from the indoor pool area. They shivered in the brisk air and wrapped towels closely around themselves, trying to keep ahold of life preservers. Some held fussy children, but most were older, holding hands and trying to stay together.

Luckily, since her cabin was near the front of the ship, her muster station wasn't very far from the bridge. That was where her luck ended. The place where her assigned lifeboat should have been hanging was empty — the lifeboat was gone.

Around her, passengers complained:

"The nerve of him. Just because he's the captain doesn't mean he can take off with our lifeboat."

"I thought the captain was supposed to go down with the ship."

"We're all gonna die!" This was from a little old lady with curly white hair that stuck out at crazy angles.

Sena looked for her classmates. They were crowded tightly at one end of the muster station, trying to remember how to put on the life vests. Some of the girls were crying, and others stared in shock. Miss Friedel, looking harried, attempted to get a headcount.

"Where are the girls in 2109?" she called.

That was Sena's room. "I'm here," she waved her hand, and scanned the group for her bunkmates. There was no sign of them.

"Charity? Paris?" called Sena. "Has anyone seen Jessica?"

"They all got massages earlier," offered a male voice. Sena turned and saw that it was Kade. "Last time I saw them they said they were going back to their room to change."

Sena was sick. Her roommates were probably lost. They had no idea where the muster station was or what to do in an emergency and it was all her fault. If she hadn't agreed to check in for them at the drill, they'd be here now.

They could die, and she'd be the one to blame.

"How long ago did you see them?" she asked Kade.

"Not long, maybe twenty minutes."

"I've got to find them," she told him.

"What if you're not back when it's time to board the lifeboats?"

Sena pointed at the empty lifeboat mount and raised an eyebrow.

"Good point. We'd better go now while Miss Frizzle

isn't looking."

The teacher spoke animatedly to a crew-member about the missing lifeboat. She insisted they find room for the kids on another lifeboat without splitting them up.

The crew-member nodded and spoke in soothing tones to Ms. Friedel, "Everything is going to be fine, it's no big deal. These kinds of things just happen sometimes when you're on a boat."

Ms. Friedel's cheeks turned red and she raised her voice in anger and disbelief. Sena thought her head might explode.

"Are you coming or what?" Sena looked over in surprise. Kade beckoned to her from a doorway leading into the ship.

"You can't come," said Sena in dismay. She didn't want to be responsible for Kade missing the lifeboat too.

Wisps of smoke trailed lazily from the open door and up into the hazy sky. "Come on, Sena, stop wasting time. Let's go."

Inside the long hallway, daylight filtered in through several windows, and people poured out of the stairwell from lower decks. When Sena got closer she saw it was completely dark below.

"No emergency lighting? This is ridiculous," said Kade.

She didn't hear him. Sena looked into the blackness and felt a wave of dizziness. Her muscles locked and her feet rooted to the floor. She was not going in there.

"Sena, hey, snap out of it."

Sena began to tremble. It was all her fault her roommates were stuck down there in the dark. She couldn't leave them. She couldn't step into that darkness either.

Her eyes found a point on the ground where the last dim light from the windows reached into the stairwell. She willed her feet to step forward to that point, but they had a mind of their own.

"What's wrong with you?" Kade snapped. "Look, I'm going after them. You can stay up here if you want."

He turned to leave, and Sena reached out to catch his arm. "No wait, I can do it. I just need a second."

Sena hesitated and he grabbed her hand. "Will you come on? I don't want to lose you in the crowd."

Her heart still beating quickly, but for a different reason now, Sena let herself be led into the darkness.

CHAPTER FOUR

THEY DESCENDED SEVERAL FLIGHTS of stairs, each smokier than the last. There were a lot of people rushing *up* the stairs, and they literally ran into a few of them. No one knew what was happening, and the sense of panic building in the darkness was ominous.

People screamed and cried and struggled to push their way up the stairs. Kade and Sena had to fight their way down, and none of the crew was anywhere in sight. A few people with flashlights on the stairs or in the hallway directing passengers where to go would have made all the difference.

She held onto Kade's hand like she was drowning and it was a lifeline. Although he probably couldn't feel his fingers anymore he didn't complain.

At the bottom of the stairs the hallway opened into a long, wide corridor and the press of people around them eased up considerably. Kade talked to her while they walked, and the sound of his voice eased the darkness that pressed in all around her. "How do you know my name?" she asked after taking a moment to gather her courage. He didn't answer immediately. She glanced at him. In the darkness she couldn't read his expression.

He gave a nervous cough. "I saw you were one of Charity's roommates."

"Oh," said Sena in a small voice. She wondered if that

was a good thing.

They counted the doors as they went until they reached her cabin. When she tried the handle, she found it was locked, and she fumbled for her keycard.

"How's that supposed to work if the power's out?"

"Hotel locks have back-up batteries. Maybe these do too." She crossed her fingers and slid the keycard into the lock. When she pulled it out, the green light flashed in the darkness and they heard the lock mechanism slide open. She grinned at Kade, though she knew he couldn't see her.

"Charity? Jessica?" she called as they went inside. The girls weren't there. It wasn't surprising, but she was still disappointed.

"Where else would they have gone?" asked Kade.

"Who knows?" Sena said, trying to think like Charity. *Shopping* was the only thing that came to mind. She felt her way toward the bed and noticed the suitcases were gone. "I think they took their stuff though. They're probably okay." That gave her an idea. "Hang on real quick." Sena climbed a few steps up the ladder to her bunk and groped in the darkness for her backpack. Inside, she rooted around until her hand closed on something small and plastic. She gave a sigh of relief and pulled out her book light. The tiny glow from the little light was as comforting as the sun.

"What do you want to do now?" asked Kade.

What Sena *wanted* was to return to the upper deck, but she had something to do first and it would probably be dangerous.

"You should go back," she told him.

"What about you?"

"I'm going down the hall a ways, then I'll be right up.

There's a fire door at the end and I want to close it."
Sena knew from the tour that the engine room was on
this deck of the ship and she wanted to do what she
could to stop the fire from spreading.

"You can't be serious. That's not your job. Let the
crew take care of it. Ms. Friedel is going to freak if we're
not back soon."

"She's going to freak anyway," said Sena, "and the
crew isn't coming." She thought of the one man whose
job it was to close all of the doors on the ship. "I've got
this, you go ahead."

"Not gonna happen," said Kade. "Let's go get this
over with."

Sena shrugged into her backpack and headed for the
back of the ship. *The stern*, she mentally corrected herself.

With every step the smoke grew thicker and more
acrid. Sena heard voices and she tried to use her book
light to see through the haze. She didn't understand what
she saw. People milled around in the hallway, tugging
suitcases out of their rooms. Children fussed and cried.
She heard a woman say, "How are we supposed to find
our way out? There's at least ten sets of emergency
stairs."

"I think we should wait for an announcement. It can't
be that bad, there's not even an alarm."

"I'm getting my camera equipment," said a man.

An elderly woman was on her knees, coughing into a
handkerchief and a little girl tried to help her to her feet.
"Please, Grandma, you've got to get up."

Sena was horrified. The engine area was nearby, and
she knew these people all had to be evacuated. She'd
witnessed a fire in her apartment building once, and
knew that some people couldn't handle emergencies.

31

They froze up and lost the ability to think straight. Like living zombies, more or less.

"Kade, we—" she turned to him and found he was already ahead of her.

He let go of her hand and shouted, "By order of the captain, all passengers are to evacuate immediately. Do not go back to your rooms. Go straight to your muster stations and wait for further instructions!"

Sena was impressed. She'd never heard Kade sound so in charge.

She moved among the people, orienting them in the right direction. "Go to the end of the hallway and take the stairs up. You can do it."

When she was certain everyone was on their way out, she headed deeper into the ship. She thought the fire door was a little ways away, and she intended to finish what she'd set out to do. Not even her fear of the dark was going to stop her.

"Sena, wait!" She turned back and her light showed Kade standing with the elderly woman in his arms, the little girl holding on to his belt loop. "Forget about the door," he said. "We've got to get out of here."

"I'll be right behind you." She gave him a push in the right direction. "You need to hurry; neither of them can handle the smoke much longer."

Kade looked at the woman he was carrying and seemed to make up his mind. "Okay, but you'd better be right behind me."

With relief, Sena watched him turn to take the woman and child to the upper deck. She was soon forced to crawl on hands and knees to find air that didn't choke her lungs. Luckily, the fire door was where she thought it was. She tugged at the large door, grunting. It was heavy and she wasn't sure she could budge it. This was a job for a trained sailor, not a scrawny fifteen-year-old girl. If the captain had taken charge of the evacuation and hadn't abandoned the ship with most of his crew, she'd be up on deck or on a lifeboat, not half-choking in the bowels of the ship.

The thought of the captain filled her with fury. He'd abandoned his own ship and left helpless elderly people and children to burn, all to save himself and his girlfriend.

Unknown reserves of strength were activated by her anger, and the door closed with a slam.

Sunlight washed over Sena when she opened the door at the top of the stairs. She looked around for Kade, disappointed not to see him. She had thought he would wait for her.

The muster station was more crowded now than it had been before, and it was difficult to make any progress through the throng of people. No one knew what to do or where to go, and the crew members she saw looked as lost and confused as the passengers.

When she got back to her group, Sena saw that all three of her bunkmates were there. Charity sat on her suitcase, one leg crossed over the other, foot tapping the air impatiently.

"Nice of you to join us," she said as Sena approached.

Sena shook her head. Charity would never change.

For the next hour or so, they waited anxiously at the muster station for the order to abandon ship. There was no word from the captain, but they saw crew members hurrying by on different tasks.

Sena's classmates were full of speculation about what

had happened as they tried to make sense of the simultaneous power outage and plane crash. The most amusing theory she heard involved a Russian jet firing on them, and the captain blasting it out of the sky with shipboard artillery.

She thought about sharing what she'd witnessed on the bridge, but doubted anyone would believe her.

They waited hour after hour, sitting on the deck and leaning on each other for support. Some of the kids sang songs, and others talked in detail about the movie *Titanic*. There were a lot of tears.

Finally, several people in crew uniforms came forward. Sena recognized Lydia from the tour earlier. Her shirt was untucked and bits of hair escaped her bun. She stepped onto a bench, raised a bullhorn and made an announcement.

"Can I please have your attention? I am Lydia, your cruise director and hostess, and I have good news. The captain has asked me to inform you that the fire we experienced in the engine room has been extinguished, and the situation on-board the *Duchess* has stabilized. There is no need to evacuate at this time."

The cheer that went up from the passengers was deafening.

Lydia waited for everyone to calm down and then went on. "Unfortunately, we're unable to bring our generators back online at this time. We ask for your patience while we recover from this unfortunate event."

Someone in the crowd shouted out, "What about food? I haven't eaten since breakfast!"

"We will be serving sandwiches on the Lido within the next few hours."

"I don't want a sandwich, I paid for the buffet!" Angry murmurs of agreement in the crowd made Sena feel sorry for Lydia. She suspected worse was yet to come.

"I also must inform you that the water pressure in the ship is not working at this time. That means you'll be unable to flush toilets or get water from the tap." She held up a red plastic bag labeled *Biohazard*. "Cabin stewards will be coming around to give you biological waste bags for your solid waste, and you can eliminate liquid waste in your showers."

Sena looked around and saw a number of confused expressions. She wasn't the only one who didn't understand. She was still trying to work out what Lydia meant when someone shouted, "I'm not gonna take a dump in a plastic bag!"

Now the crowd was really upset. It took a while before they calmed down enough to let Lydia speak again. "We need everyone's cooperation. We have our engineers working on the problem now, and we hope to have a solution by tomorrow morning. For now, we appreciate your patience."

A tall, middle-aged man with short brown hair and worry lines around his eyes spoke from the crowd. "Was anyone hurt in the fire?"

Lydia lowered the megaphone, nodded and wiped her eyes. Everyone became so still that when she spoke, they all heard her despite the lack of amplification. "Twenty people are missing, including passengers and crew. The fire spread through a section of the lower cabins before we could contain it."

There was a hush following her words, as the passengers took in the information.

When Lydia stepped down from her perch on a bench

a final question was asked. "What about the captain?"

Sena looked out toward the wreckage of the airplane. The flames had been extinguished and the rubbish that remained was just a dark blotch on the horizon.

"Staff Captain Brady has been promoted to captain. He will address everyone later tonight."

With these words, Lydia extricated herself from the crowd, and went, presumably, to deliver her bad news to another muster station.

Mr. Stoddard, the physics teacher, climbed up onto the bench and called for everyone's attention.

"Students," he paused until everyone was listening, "I think it's a good time to talk about the Compton Effect."

Groans went up all around Sena.

Mr. Stoddard went on, well accustomed to reluctant listeners. "Who can tell me what a photon is?"

No one raised their hand.

"Think of it as a tiny bundle of energy," he answered his own question. "There are lots of kinds of photons, but I want to talk about gamma rays. Gamma rays are photons with a hundred thousand times more energy than light photons."

"Can we go back to our cabins? I don't think any of us care about this right now," a student with a nose piercing and neon shoelaces spoke up.

"Do you care about what happened to the ship and that plane?" asked the teacher. He had their attention now. "Bear with me. What creates gamma rays?"

"Wasn't that what turned Bruce Banner into the Hulk?"

"Yes, exactly. What *caused* those gamma rays?"

Sena jumped in, "A nuclear reaction." All eyes turned to her for a moment and her cheeks warmed.

"Good, Sena. Now, what would happen if a nuclear weapon was detonated in space?"

Charity leaped to her feet. "That airplane was nuked?"

A loud burst of excited chatter interrupted the lecture, and Mr. Stoddard had to quiet everyone down before he could continue.

"Not exactly, Charity, but there *was* a nuclear explosion."

All eyes turned to the sky. It was a hazy blue with puffy white clouds on the horizon. Not the least bit threatening.

"It probably happened a long way away from us. Too far to notice unless you were looking in the exact right spot at the exact right moment. Miles above us, however, a nuclear bomb exploded and released a bunch of gamma rays. When the gamma rays hit the air molecules, they knocked loose a whole lot of electrons. Think of them as a flood of electrons getting pushed towards us by the blast."

Mr. Stoddard was on a roll now. He spoke quickly, motioning with his hands and running his fingers through his hair so it stood on end.

"This flood of electrons came hurtling toward the Earth's magnetic field. There, the electrons turned into a fluctuating electrical current, which in turn induced a huge, moving magnetic field, coming straight at us."

Several of the students crouched down, and Sena couldn't blame them. She wanted to hide underneath something too.

"Do we need to worry about radioactive fallout?"

Sena recognized the man who'd spoken as the one that had asked Lydia about casualties. A woman stood next to him and Sena noticed they were holding hands. The woman met Sena's eyes and gave her a small smile.

Sena looked away quickly and saw that a lot of passengers were gathered around listening to Mr. Stoddard's lecture. It was probably the most attentive class he'd ever had.

"I don't think so," answered Mr. Stoddard. "The blast was probably hundreds of miles away from us."

"What about that field thing that's coming towards us?" asked Paris. "When will it get here? Shouldn't we get inside?"

"It's already come and gone," said the teacher. "That field was what we call an Electro-Magnetic Pulse—an EMP. When it reached the surface of the Earth, it created huge electrical currents in anything that would conduct electricity. Let's take an example - everyone get your phones out." Students reached into pockets and pulled out an array of smartphones.

"Do any of them work?" asked Mr. Stoddard.

"They're all fried, man," said a boy with shaggy hair and headphones still in his ears. It was habit, probably. There obviously wasn't any music playing.

"That's right. When the electrical pulse encountered your phones, it flooded them with so much current they were instantly fried, as Jake so eloquently shared."

"Why did it catch the ship on fire though?" asked Ms. Friedel.

"I don't know exactly. My guess is that the current overwhelmed the ship's electrical infrastructure and traveled to the generator where it caused an explosion. Ship engines have always been susceptible to fire."

"And that's what happened to the plane?" asked Kade.

"That's my guess," said Mr. Stoddard. The corners of

his mouth turned down and he looked troubled. "The EMP probably disabled their engines and they couldn't get them started again."

The woman Sena noticed earlier spoke up now. "Can something like this happen by accident or be explained by natural phenomena? I've heard solar flares can cause problems similar to this."

"Solar flares might explain the power outage, though it's not likely. The sun is so far away from us it takes days for the effects of solar storms to be felt on Earth. We would have known it was coming. Additionally, a solar storm doesn't affect phones and small electronics, and it certainly wouldn't knock an airplane out of the sky. No, I'm afraid this is something much more sinister."

"What do you mean?" asked Sena.

"This was an act of war," Mr. Stoddard stated firmly. "The United States is under attack."

CHAPTER FIVE

A MAN IN A crew uniform approached Mr. Stoddard. "Excuse me, Sir? If you don't mind coming with me, I think Captain Brady needs to hear this."

Mr. Stoddard stepped down from the bench. "Will you be okay, Nancy?"

Ms. Friedel nodded. "I'll manage."

Though Lydia had said they weren't evacuating, a lot of the people at the muster station stayed where they were, reluctant to leave.

Sena didn't have anywhere else to go. Her cabin was too dark and smoky, the deck was crowded, and though it was well past lunchtime, there was no food. She wished she'd thought to bring some snacks for the trip, or at least some water, but with buffets available all day every day, food had been the last thing she thought she'd have to worry about.

Standing at the rail, she scanned the horizon for the lifeboat with the captain and crew. The floating wreckage of the plane caught her eye and she thought about where the plane might have been heading. A sudden realization caused her knees to weaken, and she clutched the rail of the ship for support. Her foster family had been in a plane on their way to California.

Could the effects of the EMP extend that far? She thought of the terror they would have experienced when the plane's engines stopped in midair and the plane began to lose altitude. People would have been screaming and crying. Tears filled her eyes at the thought of Jamie and Tessa in that situation. They were so little. She hadn't formed a close bond with her foster parents, though she loved their kids.

She also wondered what had happened to her real mom. Was she still in prison? She'd been due for parole. Had she made it out before the attack? Sena couldn't help but think of the terror and danger of being in a place like that and suddenly having the power go off.

Please let her be somewhere safe.

Tears dripped down her cheeks and off the end of her chin, insignificant drops of saltwater mingling with the vast ocean below.

She heard laughter behind her and wiped her eyes, then turned to look. Her roommates were flirting with a group of guys. Kade was there too.

How could they joke around when the world was ending?

Kade laughed at someone's joke and for a moment their eyes met. His face was smiling while his eyes were sad. Maybe people dealt with things in different ways. Sena turned back to look at the ocean. She stood there a long time, alone.

A sailor announced that dinner was being served on the Lido, so Sena and a group of students headed straight over, dismayed with what they found. The line for the food stretched all the way from the Grand Buffet, circled the pool area, and then curved back past the other side of the buffet and clear to the opposite end of the ship.

"I'm going to go see what the deal is," said Kade. He was gone a while, and when he came back he shrugged. "It's only sandwiches, I'm sure the line will move fast."

That had been over two hours ago.

Charity and Paris had long since vanished, making excuses about the bathroom and telling Sena to get something for them in case they weren't back in time.

Sena read her library book in line, glad she had her backpack and wouldn't have to return to the room. Although she wasn't sure where she was going to sleep, she had no desire to go back down into the smoky darkness below decks.

By the time the students finally reached the serving area at the front of the line, all of the lunchmeat for the sandwiches was gone. Sena learned that previous passengers had piled their sandwiches with enough meat and cheese for five or six sandwiches, worried there wouldn't be any more food. A young Filipino serving girl gestured to the students to take a sandwich roll and fill it with tomatoes and onions.

After all Sena had been through, this was the final straw. She had *seen* how much food was on the ship, and the thought of eating an onion sandwich for dinner filled her with helpless anger. Why didn't the chef send up more food? The refrigerators were bursting with it.

Several people were already yelling at the serving girl, who looked thoroughly miserable. Sena knew it wasn't her fault, and suppressed the urge to join in. Instead, she took her roll and two more for Charity and Paris, along with a bottle of water, and then stormed away from the pool area and found an unclaimed bench with a view of the water. If anyone looked like they were about to sit next to her, she would shrivel them with one look.

She ate her roll and then, feeling rebellious, ate the rolls she'd gotten for her bunkmates too. If they wanted to eat they could stand in line like everyone else.

Someone sat next to her on the bench and she was about to order them away when she saw it was Danny, the serving boy she'd met briefly the day before.

"I thought it was you," he said with a tired smile. He looked exhausted. His soot covered face was streaked with perspiration and he reeked of smoke.

"What happened to you?" she cried, her anger gone as quickly as it had come.

"Wrong place, wrong time," he said. "I'd taken lunch down to engineering when the power went out. Did you hear the explosion?"

Sena shook her head. "I was up on the bridge. I saw the captain try to contact you, but the call wouldn't go through."

"Yeah, we never got it. It was crazy down there. After the explosion everything went dark and people were screaming and running all over. A lot of the crew took off." Danny's eyebrows knit together and Sena had no doubt what he thought about that.

"Were you scared?"

"I didn't have time to be. It was pitch black and the sprinklers didn't kick in. I thought we were goners for sure. Chief Huang never lost his cool though. Do you know he's got a back-up hand pump down there? It's older than he is. He asked for it special when the ship used to have a big fish tank. He said it was to pump seawater in for the tank, but he told me he actually got it for emergencies. Smart guy. Between that and the fire extinguishers, we were able to get things under control." He paused, and Sena heard the heaviness in his voice

43

when he added, "Just not fast enough."

Sena tried to sound comforting. "You did everything you could."

"The fire broke out into a couple of cabin areas. There were a few families on the one side that hadn't gone topside in time. They didn't make it." He paused. "I swear we had someone looking out for us today though. The other area was evacuated and sealed off. Whoever had the presence of mind to close that door probably saved a few lives. Maybe more than a few."

Sena worked hard to swallow around the lump in her throat.

"You can't know that," she finally said.

"Well I'll tell you what I do know," said Danny. "Half the crew is hiding below decks. Someone told them the captain took off with all the officers and they figure they're going to lose their jobs when we get back to port anyway, so why deal with the angry Americans?" He shook his head. "Someone will probably be here by tomorrow to tug us back to Seattle. We're only a day out; we can keep things running that long."

"I don't think anyone is coming." Sena told him what she'd seen on the bridge, and then what the physics teacher had told them about EMPs.

Danny whistled under his breath. "Guess I can forget about Alaska. If what you said is true, we'll be lucky to make it back home at all."

"Can't they fix the engines?" asked Sena. "Enough to get us ashore?"

He shook his head. "From what I heard, if they try to restart them it might cause a spark and the whole thing could go up again. We're stuck out here, and we're going to get low on food real fast."

"No way," said Sena. "You should see how much food they've got down there."

"It might seem like a lot, but think about it," said Danny. "How many days to Alaska?"

"Six."

"Do you think the chef stocked up with more food than we'd need?"

Sena remembered the efficiency of the food inventory system. "No."

"So we have six days of food at most, right?"

"We could stretch it a little if we don't eat as much. It's not like we need buffets all day and all night." *We could eat onion sandwiches*.

"If we had six days of pre-cooked food, that would be one thing, but most of the supplies require prep, and it's so dark down there they can't *see* the food, let alone cook it."

Sena recalled how the bread was baked fresh every day and most of the meat was frozen. Even if they ate salad three times a day, who was going to wash three thousand dishes by hand after every meal? It wasn't like the ship had a bunch of paper plates. Or water.

"Oh my gosh," said Sena as a thought occurred to her. "Food isn't the problem. It's water."

Danny tilted his head, "How so?"

"There's not enough water onboard to get us to Alaska. There's only about half as much as we need in back-up tanks, and for the rest, the ship has its own de-salinization plant. I learned about it on my tour of the ship this morning." Morning felt like a lifetime ago. "It pretty much makes its own water as we go. I doubt the plant will work without power though."

"Unless the Chief can rig something up, we can't get

water from the tanks either. There's no pressure or pumps to bring it out."

"This is crazy! How can they not be more prepared for something like this?" exclaimed Sena. "We can't be the first ship to lose power away from land."

"No, we're the first ship to lose primary power, back-up power, radio, radar, satellite communications, and our captain all at the same time."

The seriousness of their situation silenced both of them until Sena finally asked, "What do you think's going to happen?"

"Maybe the Navy has ships that are still okay. All we need is a tug back to Seattle and we can get everyone home. It's not that far."

Despite Danny's optimistic words, she could see the doubt in his eyes. He stood up.

"Hey, I'd better get going. You'll never guess what they've got me doing tomorrow. Did you see the red bags they were giving out? Well, someone has to go around and pick them up."

Sena wrinkled her nose. "Ew! They shouldn't make you do that, you're a hero!"

Danny gave a shrug, "I volunteered. I couldn't pass up the chance to be able to say I've done doody duty."

Sena groaned and shook her head as he walked away.

CHAPTER SIX

SENA LOOKED AROUND, SURPRISED not to see more people. She was on one of the uppermost decks in an outdoor theater. The sun was sinking quickly, painting the sky a brilliant orange where the fiery water reached up to lap at the horizon. A chilly breeze blew across the deck and she shivered, despite her long-sleeved shirt and pants. Hopefully the captain would start soon.

She sat with Ms. Friedel and most of her classmates. A few had opted to stay with their things and reserve their sleeping area. The class had claimed a large atrium that opened to the main casino. When the ship had power it was a stunning area, with a high open ceiling that stretched up three floors to an enormous chandelier made of blue sheets of glass. There were stairs with wrought-iron railings at both ends of the lobby and a grand piano graced the center of the room.

The teachers thought the students had chosen it because there were a lot of couches and comfortable chairs. Sena knew it was because of the secluded alcoves and near total darkness. There weren't any windows in the atrium and she imagined there'd be plenty of who-knew-what going on that night.

As for Sena, she would be sleeping on deck where there was some light. She didn't care how cold it got. Even if there wasn't a moon that night, there would be stars.

She turned her attention to the stage, where Captain Brady was about to speak. He wore a white dress uniform and captain's hat. He didn't look tired, though she was sure he must be. When he spoke, his voice carried to the whole theater over the sound of the waves lapping against the boat.

"Tonight, you are seated with heroes. Look around and you will see brave men and women, both crew and passengers, that went beyond what they had to do today, at times risking their own lives. Without them—without you—we wouldn't be here tonight. I thank you, and I honor you.

"Many of our shipmates aren't here tonight. I can't speak for all of them, but my training leads me to believe that a lot of them are overwhelmed by the circumstances we face. In a crisis situation, people tend to freeze up or shut down. They may become angry or depressed. I ask you to be patient with them, and help where you can.

"Luxury services will no longer be available. In these emergency circumstances I cannot in good faith ask the staff to continue to provide you with full-service and amenities. You may even be asked to pitch in. We will need everyone's help to get through this.

"I'm not going to lie to you, we're in a very serious situation. We were able to use a battery-operated satellite phone to make contact with the Navy in Hawaii. They are still trying to get a full assessment of the extent of the damage, but early reports indicate that power and communications have been disrupted for all of the West Coast."

A loud murmur arose from the crowd, and it wasn't until then that Sena realized how bad the situation could be. Who was behind the attack? Was a war going on somewhere at this very minute?

The captain raised his hands, and when the crowd quieted he spoke again. "What we experienced today goes beyond the boundaries of this ship. Navy resources are stretched thin and we can't anticipate outside help. The commanding officers and I are making plans to get everyone safely back to shore in Seattle. Right now we ask for your patience and tolerance. You are the heroes of the day, and we need you to continue to be leaders to your fellow passengers. Help us keep people safe and calm until we are ready to act, and be assured that we do have a plan to get you home. Thank you and God bless you."

The captain left the stage, and one of the ship's performers took his place. Sena pondered what kind of show they were about to see, sure no one was in the mood for entertainment.

The thin slip of a girl stepped forward to stand at the edge of the stage and began to sing in a stronger voice than Sena had expected.

"Oh, say can you see, by the dawn's early light…"

As if of one accord, the crowd rose to its feet, removing hats, placing hands over hearts.

Sena stood and tried to sing along, her throat tight with emotion. The song had greater meaning for her tonight than it ever had. Now they too, faced a long, dark night in a time of war, not knowing what the future would bring.

After the song was over, Sena wiped her eyes and slipped away before the crowd dispersed and Ms. Friedel could round her up with the other students. It was almost full dark and she wanted to be safely on her bench before the last light of the sun faded from the sky.

To her dismay, an elderly man had claimed the bench while she was gone so Sena was forced to find another place to sleep.

She stood in the middle of the Lido deck and looked around. All of the pool chairs were taken, and most of the deck space was covered by mattresses that had been removed from beds and dragged to the open air. Without power for ventilation, the rooms below decks were basically uninhabitable, stuffy and clogged with smoke. Sena sat forlornly on a stool at the tequila bar, and had the random thought that she'd expected her first time at a bar would be more thrilling.

Nothing was being served now, and the seats would be too uncomfortable to sleep in, but the area was lit by small, solar powered lights, so a few people congregated there. A woman sat on the stool next to Sena's and fiddled with her ruined phone.

"I feel like I don't know what to do with my hands anymore," she said when she noticed Sena watching her. "Maybe I'll take up smoking." The woman laughed, and Sena saw in the dim light that the smile didn't reach her eyes. "I wish I'd brought a picture of my kids. I had plenty in my phone but now…"

Sena thought she recognized her from the muster station earlier. "How many kids do you have?" she asked, trying to be polite.

"Two. Well, one living. My son died a year ago."

Sena didn't know what to say. *Sorry* sounded so trite. Without thinking, she said the first thing that came to mind. "I lost my mom a few years ago too. I mean, she didn't die, but she went to jail for letting her boyfriend cook meth in our kitchen."

Sena was horrified at herself for what she'd just said. She never talked about that, not with anyone.

The woman nodded and took it in stride. "That must have been hard."

"She made parole, and as soon as I get home she wants me to move back in with her. We'll be a family again."

"I hope things work out with you and your mom. Family is important."

The conversation fizzled and Sena was sure she'd said too much. People got uncomfortable when she talked about her past so she'd learned not to bring it up. She wasn't sure why she'd broken her rule tonight. It always made things awkward.

To her surprise, the woman still wanted to talk. "I noticed you earlier today. I bet you're about my daughter's age. What are you, fourteen, fifteen?"

"Fifteen."

"Maddie's fifteen too. Dee, I mean. That's what she likes to be called. I'm Claire."

The woman looked at Sena, obviously waiting.

My name is Sena."

"Sena. That's a pretty name. I don't think I've ever heard it."

"It's Korean. I was named after my mom's mom."

"I bet that meant a lot to your grandmother. Do you have a Korean last name too?"

"No, it's Morgan, after my dad. He died in Iraq before I was born. My parents weren't married or anything, but my mom still wanted me to have his name, so I'm Sena Morgan."

They lapsed into silence again and although Sena was reluctant to leave the oasis of light, she was afraid of what she might blurt out next. Talking to Claire came too easily.

Sena stood to leave, and couldn't help noticing the deep shadows outside the tequila bar. "I better get going."

"Hold on, I was thinking... we've got a cabin on this deck, my husband and I. If you don't have somewhere to sleep you're welcome to our couch. I haven't checked, but I think it might fold out to a bed."

"Oh, I couldn't impose on you. You don't even know me."

"I know you're a kid on her own in the middle of the ocean. Everyone needs a break sometimes." Claire touched Sena lightly on the arm. "Let me help you."

Sena bit her lip to hide the quiver. It had been so long since someone had done something motherly for her.

Claire mistook her silence for refusal and went on. "When I said goodbye to my daughter yesterday she was barely speaking to me. After today I wish I could go back and hug her and tell her I'm sorry. I can't, but I can give someone else's daughter a safe place to sleep."

Sena looked into Claire's face and saw kindness and sincerity. Her daughter probably had no idea how lucky she was.

"All right, I'll try it, thank you."

It was too dark to see the cabin very well, though Sena was too tired to care. The couch was soft and she fell asleep within minutes, clutching her book light and barely noticing when Claire gently tucked a blanket around her shoulders and hummed a wordless lullaby.

Breakfast the next morning was simple and plentiful: cold slices of ham, fresh fruit and milk. The serving staff had learned their lesson the day before and were providing breakfast on two decks. Not only that, they served the food themselves instead of letting passengers get their own. Second helpings were allowed; to get them you had to go through the line again. The lines were much shorter and everyone seemed to be getting enough to eat.

After breakfast, Claire gave her a room key and told Sena she was welcome any time. Sena thanked her, and said she might stop by again sometime.

The day stretched out ahead of her and she thought about what to do with her time. The two main decks were crowded with mattresses and makeshift tents made from bed sheets. People were crammed into every corner and it was far too crowded for her comfort. She thought about looking for Danny to see if he needed help with anything, but then remembered his doody duties and decided he was on his own.

She pulled her map of the ship out of her backpack and scanned it, hoping for inspiration. Suddenly something caught her eye and she grinned.

The ship had a library.

Sena re-shelved the book she'd been reading and sank down into a chair with a happy sigh. She'd spent the last couple of hours engrossed in a zombie story about the end of the world. She wanted to tell the author that zombies were out, EMPs were in.

She was trying to decide what to do next when Kade walked in. He paused in the doorway, sunshine from the skylight making his hair look blonder than it actually was. When he spotted her he walked over.

"I didn't think I'd see you here. Is this where you

slept?"

Sena shook her head.

"You weren't downstairs were you? The Frizz assigned everyone to specific areas and went half-crazy when she kept coming up one kid short. I hope you don't mind – I told her you had a thing about the dark and were probably on a pool chair somewhere."

"Thanks, I didn't mean to worry her. I didn't think anyone would notice."

"I noticed."

Sena looked away and pushed her glasses up higher on her nose. She didn't know what to say. She couldn't read Kade at all. One minute he was nice and the next he ignored her.

"What are you doing here?" she said.

"You don't think I like books?"

Sena bit her lip, raised her eyebrows and looked sideways.

He laughed. "Okay, you got me. I was just roaming and figured I'd check it out." He reached into his pocket and pulled out a handful of batteries. "Hey," he said, "I've got something for you."

"Um, thanks?"

"You don't know what they're for, do you? Your book light. Duh."

Sena stared at the batteries, in shock that he'd done something so thoughtful. For her. "How did you get so many?"

"I scavenged them out of a couple of TV remotes. I figured they might come in handy. It's no big deal."

Sena looked at the batteries and back at Kade. "Are you kidding? It's huge!"

"Seriously, it's nothing. What time are you going to

head down for dinner?"

"What time is it?" Sena tucked the batteries into her backpack, enjoying the sense of security they gave her.

Kade squinted at the sun through the library's large windows. "Um, no idea? My stomach's telling me it's after lunch though. Two meals a day is rough on a guy."

He was referring to the announcement posted on the main bulletin board that the number of meals served had been reduced to two, one in the morning and one in the evening. The new meal schedule was very unpopular.

Kade plopped into the chair next to hers and they stared out at the vast ocean. Sena tried to think of something to talk about. She wondered briefly why it was so much easier to talk to Danny than to Kade. She didn't know him as well, but when they talked she felt smart and witty. With Kade she mostly felt awkward.

She glanced over at him to see if he looked as uncomfortable as she felt. He was squinting out the window. "Do you see something out there?" he asked, pointing.

Sena pushed up her glasses and leaned forward to get a better look. "A lot of wat—" she began, cutting herself off when she spotted a tiny speck.

"I think you're right!" she said excitedly. "Do you think it's a ship?"

"Could be. A distant ship, or smoke on the horizon."

"Smoke?"

"Never mind, I was just… never mind."

"Do you think the Navy sent someone to get us?"

"Could be. We'd better go tell the captain. Do you know the way to the bridge?"

Sena nodded. "Come on."

* * *

Sena was surprised when they were permitted to join the captain on the bridge. Captain Brady stood up when he saw her and took her hand in a firm handshake.

"Sena Morgan, right? From what I've been told, you explicitly went against my orders and helped evacuate passengers on the Riviera Deck during the fire. You're not very good at following orders, young lady."

Sena was reminded of how she felt when the security guard at the hotel caught her pilfering food. She wished she could shrink away to nothing.

"Lucky thing for us."

He caught her eye and she could see the hint of a smile. She let herself relax a little.

"I presume this is Kade Miller?" He shook Kade's hand. "I'm glad you both stopped by, I wanted to thank you in person. I heard from several sources about your bravery. Without your presence of mind in helping evacuate the area, things could have been a whole lot worse."

He turned to face the long windows and Sena was secretly gratified when he pulled a small telescope out of his pocket and looked through it. He was the perfect image of a sailor.

"I hear you noticed something out there. Would you like to get a better look?"

Kade nodded and was handed the telescope. He looked for a moment and then gave it to Sena.

Through the telescope, the tiny speck resolved into a small watercraft. It wasn't big enough to be called a ship, though it looked bigger than a sailboat.

"I think it's getting closer," she said, studying it intently.

"That's correct," said Captain Brady. "We'll have

company before long. Does it look familiar?"

"Not really, should it?" asked Kade.

A flash of color caught Sena's eye and she gasped.

"What is it?" asked Kade.

"I think Ms. Morgan has recognized the boat."

Sena handed the telescope to the Kade with a heavy heart.

"Oh no," said Kade.

"Oh yes," said the captain. "It would appear the prodigal has returned. Our former captain will be rejoining us shortly."

CHAPTER SEVEN

"YOU'RE NOT GOING TO let him back on the *Duchess*, are you?" Sena asked. He *deserved* to go straight to the brig, in her opinion.

"I'd rather not," said Captain Brady. "I don't think we have a choice though. Attempts to restore power have been unsuccessful, and if we have to use the lifeboats to get us safely ashore we will need their boat as well. I can't allow myself to harbor a grudge."

"He took off in our lifeboat and left us to die," Sena insisted. "I think it's okay to hold a grudge."

"The lives of my passengers must come first. Now, if you'll excuse us, the crew and I have a few things to discuss."

Kade and Sena found a spot at the railing near the prow of the ship where they could see the lifeboat approach.

"You know," said Kade, "if I was that scumbag, you couldn't pay me enough to come back to the *Duchess*. He has to know we all hate him."

Though she despised him for his cowardice, Sena was surprised to find she didn't actually hate the captain. She wasn't sure how she would have reacted in the same situation. If Kade hadn't been with her when she'd tried to go into the darkened ship to look for her bunkmates, she wasn't sure she could have done it. Captain Crane was wrong to leave, however, he was still human.

The lifeboat was white with a bright orange cover that made it look like a plastic version of Noah's ark. Captain Crane's head and shoulders were visible. He was standing in an opening near the back of the vessel and directing it to the pilot's ladder at the bottom of the ship just behind where the bow cut through the water.

The captain struggled to maneuver the lifeboat into position in the choppy sea. He took a rope, leaped from the boat, and swam to the ship. He secured the lifeboat to the cruise ship, and then reached the pilot's ladder and began the long climb to the deck.

Sena noted that she and Kade had been joined by Captain Brady and the commanding officers of the ship. He nodded to her and then turned his attention to the man climbing over the railing.

"Welcome back," said Captain Brady. "You can remain in your lifeboat moored to the ship. If you or the other officers wish to come aboard I'll have to detain you in the brig."

"Not so fast," said Crane.

"You abandoned the ship; that's a major offense. You're guilty of a crime."

"You know full well we didn't abandon the ship. We left on a rescue mission."

Captain Brady snorted.

"I have proof," said Crane. "The rescue operation was successful. We have several survivors from the plane in need of medical attention."

"What? You're saying someone actually survived that crash?" Captain Brady said, immediately dropping his formal tone.

"Quite a few, actually. We found them on a life raft."

"Near the crash site?"

"Near enough."

"How many?"

"There are eleven survivors."

"And you say some are injured? How badly?"

"Burns, mostly."

Captain Brady turned to an officer and gave orders to prepare boarding assistance for the wounded, and then addressed the deserter once more.

"In light of these discoveries, I will rethink your sentence."

"My sentence? Are you kidding? I'm a hero!"

"You'll be confined to quarters until we reach a decision."

When Crane opened his mouth to protested, Captain Brady cut him off. "Do you see these people? You'll stand trial for your crimes against them."

Passengers had gathered on many levels to watch the scene unfold. Sena wasn't sure why she'd been allowed to stay; now she understood that Captain Brady had needed an audience.

At the sight of the angry faces, some of the wind went out of Crane's sails. Sena was close enough to hear his quietly spoken words, "Listen, Brady, I know I screwed up. I came back to make it right. If you give me another chance, I'll prove it to you. That's all I'm asking for. Just one more chance."

"We'll see," said Captain Brady.

"One last thing," said Crane in a low voice. "Keep an eye on the survivors. I'm not sure I trust them."

With that mysterious statement, he allowed himself to be led from sight.

* * *

The line for dinner that night was almost two hours long, most likely because word got out there was chocolate pudding. They were also serving canned cocktail shrimp with cocktail sauce, smoked salmon wraps, and salad. Time in line passed quickly, because everyone wanted to talk about the return of Captain Crane.

Sena was surprised by how many passengers believed he should be reinstated as captain. They said he was a hero for taking immediate action and rescuing the survivors of the plane crash. Could it be possible she wasn't giving him enough credit?

Sena poked at a wilted lettuce leaf that she supposed might qualify as "salad," and considered. She thought back to Crane's flippant dismissal of the plane crash victims as "rotisserie chicken." At that moment he clearly didn't have the least intention of attempting a rescue. It wasn't until he heard about the serious state of his own ship that he'd decided to leave. The man was either a coward or terribly selfish. Maybe both, but definitely not a hero.

What surprised her was that he'd actually gone to the crash site to look for survivors. She would have expected him to make a beeline straight for land. Was there more to his story? And why had he come back?

Though the salad may have been wilted, the chocolate pudding was delicious. Everything had been served on the same plate, and she'd had to eat the pudding with a fork. At least the chefs were still managing to put together two meals each day.

She was putting her plate and fork in the bin when she heard a voice she recognized.

"Man, am I glad to see you!" Danny's tone was simultaneously happy and relieved. "They've got me taking dessert down to the new arrivals in the medical center. I tried to get someone else to do it, but everyone's either hiding out or running food for dinner. There was a dishwasher who offered to trade with me but I do have some self-respect."

"What's wrong with the new arrivals?" asked Sena.

"Oh, nothing, I'm sure. I've got a thing about hospitals and doctors." He set the tray down so he could untie his apron. "Put this on over your clothes. Things are so crazy around here, no one will notice." Danny deftly slipped the apron over her head before she could object.

Angry tears sprang to Sena's eyes and she flushed. What if she didn't *want* to go down into the dark below deck area? She would expect a stunt like this from her classmates, not from Danny.

"There now, don't you look..." Danny trailed off when he saw her face. "Oh man, I really screwed that up, didn't I?"

Sena blinked rapidly, mortified that she was on the verge of tears over something so stupid. She turned away to swipe at her glasses with the apron.

"I kind of hate myself right now," said Danny. He whisked the apron away from her like it was a magician's tablecloth. "Can I start over? I'll give you my best Bambi eyes."

Danny's Bambi impression was as unfortunate as it was adorable and Sena couldn't stay mad at him.

"What I meant to say is they're making me take these puddings down to the medical center and I'm terrified of doctors. Would you mind coming along to give me moral support?"

Sena didn't think anyone had ever bothered to apologize to her when they'd hurt her feelings. She was charmed and decided right there that she'd go with him to the depths of the sea. Well, maybe not the depths. It was pretty dark down there.

"Give me the apron," she said, holding out a hand and putting it on herself this time. "You're carrying the tray though."

There was a brief moment of indecision for Sena when they came to the stairs, but when Danny opened the door she saw the stairwell was lit by glow-sticks. It was enough light for her to manage. The medical center was on the same level as most of the food storage, and Sena was surprised that there weren't any guards at the crew-only door leading to the large refrigerators.

She realized most of the passengers probably had no idea what was inside, since staff-only elevators and stairways kept them oblivious to the way food was moved through the ship. Sena only knew because she'd taken the ship tour.

This was only a passing thought, as a more uncomfortable effect of the power outage was bothering her. Lydia, the cruise director, had explained earlier that without power, the ship's stabilizers would no longer keep the boat perfectly level so they were likely to notice a tilt, or list.

Sena sure noticed it now. Walking in a straight line was difficult, and Danny was having trouble balancing the tray. The puddings slid from one side to the other and she was sure they were going to go right over the edge. She reached out to catch one, and then noticed

Danny's enormous grin.

She punched him in the arm not holding the tray. "You're making them slide on purpose!"

"You're fun to mess with, you know that?" He tilted the tray again and really did almost lose one of the cups over the edge. "These sure look good," he said, looking at the little bowls. "There's a baby photo of me somewhere eating a bowl of chocolate pudding. You should see the mess I made."

Sena saw a mischievous glint in Danny's eyes. "You wouldn't dare!"

"Wouldn't dare what?" he said with feigned innocence and painted a streak of chocolate pudding on her cheek.

Sena shrieked, "You're going to get it!"

"Is there a problem out here?" A woman in mint-green scrubs stuck her head out of one of the doors and Sena realized they'd reached the infirmary. Danny deftly stepped behind her at the sight of the nurse, so Sena was left to do the talking.

"We brought some dessert for the new arrivals."

"Ah, yes. Follow me. We've got so many patients right now we had to put them in a conference room."

It was only a few steps down the hall, and she held the door for Sena and Danny to enter.

"You've got something on your cheek, by the way."

Sena felt a blush spread over her face, and scrubbed at the pudding with the apron.

Once her face was clean, Sena looked around the conference room. Electric lights were on. It was the best lit area she'd seen since the power went out. The hum of an emergency generator revealed the source of the power operating the lights and various pieces of medical equipment in the room.

Danny saw Sena gaping and whispered, "They put one in the main galley too. Captain Brady was offered the third, but he turned it down. Said all the equipment on the bridge was burned out anyway. I think they've got it in the engine room now."

Beds lined the entire room, and the new passengers were grouped together in one corner of the room. Most of them wore blue jumpsuits.

"Did we run out of hospital gowns?" asked Danny.

"No," said the nurse. "That's what they were wearing when they boarded."

"Oh," he said. "Weird."

It *was* kind of weird, now that he'd mentioned it. Maybe the clothes were part of the emergency supplies on the lifeboat.

"Come on, let's get this over with," Danny whispered.

Sena wasn't in a hurry; she was fascinated by the survivors. They'd survived a plane crash, and then, against all odds, been rescued at sea. Not only that, but they looked Korean. Her grandmother was part Korean and when Sena lived with her she'd spoken Korean at home. Even though she didn't remember much of it anymore, she could still say a few things. She decided to try hello.

"Annyeong-hasimnikka."

Several pairs of unfriendly eyes turned her way and a surge of embarrassment washed over her. Was she wrong about them being Korean? Had she just insulted them?

"Did you ask them to walk the plank or something?" Danny asked.

"It seems like it."

"Here, maybe some pudding will cheer them up." Danny handed her a cup and Sena tried to give it to one

65

of the men. He refused to take it, or even to make eye contact with her.

"Try the next guy."

The Korean in the blue jumpsuit didn't look her straight in the eye. He gazed at a point a little over her shoulder, like he could see someone sneaking up behind her. It gave her the creeps, and she had to will herself not to turn to see what he was looking at.

In the end, none of the men would take the dessert.

"All the more for me," said Danny brightly in an obvious attempt to lighten the mood.

"I guess," said Sena, troubled. Maybe they had post-traumatic stress syndrome. They'd certainly been through enough. She turned to leave and then froze when one of the men said something to her in Korean. She told herself she'd heard him wrong, but his whispered words were spoken with such malice, she knew she'd understood.

She took Danny's hand and walked quickly to the door, the menacing words still ringing in her ears.

"We will kill you all."

CHAPTER EIGHT

"YOU MUST HAVE HEARD him wrong," Danny said, after making her explain why she'd practically dragged him out of the room.

"I guess," said Sena. It *had* been a long time since she'd heard any Korean. And why would the men have any reason to want to hurt them? Regardless, his tone still echoed in her head and creeped her out.

Danny and Sena turned at the sound of footsteps in the hallway and Sena recognized Captain Brady and Chief Engineer Huang.

"Visiting the survivors, I see," said the captain. "I hear they're not very talkative."

Sena shook her head, contemplating whether she should mention what she'd heard.

"Captain Crane said the same thing. Said they kept to themselves on the lifeboat too."

"You called him 'captain.' Does that mean you're reinstating him?" Danny asked. "He's a good man," he added.

"No, habit, I guess. He *is* a good man, but he's going to have to face a Board of Inquiry before he can captain a ship again. I know there's a faction that wants him reinstated, however, maritime law is clear. Regardless of the reasons for his leaving," the captain met Danny's look, "there's no question that he left the ship in a crisis situation. Bringing back the survivors may or may not help his case. I won't speculate; that's for the Board to decide. How are they, anyway? The survivors, I mean."

Danny looked to Sena. She took a deep breath and said, "I think they might be trouble."

The captain raised his brows in a questioning look.

She hurried on before she lost her nerve. "Are we sure the plane crashed because of an EMP? And why are they all wearing the same thing? I think they might be hijackers."

The captain shook his head. "I doubt that. Maybe union workers headed to a job. I don't want you to worry about it too much. We'll get this sorted out. Now, I'm sure this young man needs his apron so he can get back to work." Captain Brady emphasized *back to work* in a way that made Danny shift uncomfortably.

"And Ms. Morgan, you should join the scavenger hunt Lydia set up for the teens on the Lido. Everyone who participates gets a can of Coke."

"Cold?" asked Danny.

"Now that *would* be a prize," said the captain, before entering the medical center.

Back on the upper deck, the sun was slowly sinking toward the horizon and Danny left Sena to go find out what his next assignment was. Sena wasn't interested in participating in a scavenger hunt, so she wandered the deck, going wherever her fancy took her. She was surprised to see one of the ship's gift shops was open and went inside to look around. It was pretty typical fare— key rings, coffee mugs and photo frames. The bookshelves were almost bare though. With no computers or tablets to occupy them, people were reading more books and magazines. The puzzles were sold out too.

She picked up a toy cruise ship that you could pull back and release to make it roll across the floor on its own. Her foster sister would love it.

A moment later Sena's smile faded, and with a heavy heart she placed it back on the shelf. Her foster family was gone. Where would she go when they got back to shore? Maybe to find her mother?

On her way out, Sena noticed the disposable cameras were almost sold out. *Makes sense*, she thought, since camera phones and digital cameras no longer worked. She decided she'd get one too, and document life on a stranded cruise ship. Maybe she could write a book about the experience someday.

They only had waterproof cameras left, and they were slightly more expensive, but she had enough cash for one, and thought it would be fun to experiment with a few underwater photos.

With the camera in hand, she became fascinated by what the other passengers were doing. One level up from the Lido was the Panorama Deck where the captain had addressed the passengers from the open air stage.

Mattresses and blankets covered almost every inch of the deck, with only a few narrow pathways left for walking. Sheets were rigged to form barriers when possible, giving a sense of privacy for a few. It was cold at night, and they were lucky so far that it hadn't rained, but it was better than being in the staterooms on the lower decks.

She snapped a few photos of the transformation of the deck, and then turned her camera on the people.

Sena had always heard that tragedy brought out the

worst in people. She'd believed it, based on the rioting and destruction she'd seen on videos at school of post-disaster areas. That's what happened in most of the zombie books she'd read too. It was always every man for himself.

That wasn't what was happening on the ship though. Yes, a few people were difficult, still complaining about the onion sandwiches from the first day, or the red bags that everyone had learned to hate. However, most of the passengers were friendly and helpful to each other.

As she walked through the makeshift tent city she took a picture of a group doing Bible study and another of a man with a guitar leading a sing-along. She saw couples offer their cabins to parents with young children, and teens offer to wait in the food lines for elderly people. Everywhere she looked she saw kindness and charity, and it made her proud.

She realized it had been a while since she'd seen Charity, and wondered how her bunkmate was dealing with everything. She decided to look for her.

Charity was on the Lido Deck, curled up in a big towel on one of the pool chairs, shivering. *Click.* A moment frozen in time.

"Oh, hi," she said when Sena sat down next to her.

"Are you okay?" asked Sena, pressing a hand to her forehead, worried she might have a fever. The last thing they needed right now with no working toilets was an outbreak of rotavirus. It was unthinkable.

"Yeah," said Charity. "Jessica dared me to go in the pool. I didn't think it would be so cold." Her teeth chattered and Sena could barely make out what she was saying. "It's cold downstairs too, and stuffy. I figured at least up here I could breathe."

"Where did Jessica go?"

"I don't know. I think there's supposed to be a dance a little bit later, and there are rumors they're opening the bar. She probably went to get ready."

"I somehow doubt Ms. Friedel is going to let her go to open bar night."

"The Frizz won't know. The teachers are in over their heads. No one wants to hang out below, and they can't keep track of everyone coming and going."

"Don't you want to go?"

"I guess not," Charity said, her voice trembling slightly. "I keep thinking about my family back in Seattle, you know?"

Sena did know. She'd been very carefully avoiding all thoughts of her foster family's flight to California.

"It's hard to party when so many bad things are probably happening back home."

Sena found herself surprised that Charity was capable of thinking beyond the next social event, and then immediately felt bad for thinking so harshly of the girl. The truth was, they barely knew each other.

"If you want, you can share my cabin tonight," Sena surprised herself by offering.

"You've got a cabin?"

"Well, it belongs to a married couple… they're letting me crash on their couch. It's a hide-a-bed if you want to share."

"That sounds pretty good," said Charity. "I thought a great big slumber party with the whole class would be a blast. It wasn't. It was kind of sad. A lot of crying, more than anything."

"I can't promise no crying, but it will be more comfortable than the floor."

71

"You're on," said Charity and stood up. She bent down to get something and Sena realized she had her suitcase.

"Do you take that with you everywhere?"

"Pretty much," said Charity. "Which way is the cabin? Does it have a balcony?"

Sena led the way, hoping she hadn't just made a big mistake.

Claire and her husband were happy to share their room with Charity, and they sat in the semi-darkness for a while, talking about home and families. Claire's husband was named Ted, and they were visiting from Maryland. Ted was a government contractor and he wasn't optimistic about their chances of getting military help.

"You think the military's electronics are fried too?" asked Charity.

"They've known about the threat of EMP for years and never took it seriously. I think we're in a world of trouble."

"All right, well we should probably get to sleep," said Claire. "It's getting dark."

In the fading light they made the couch into a bed, and Sena laid down facing away from Charity. She turned on her book light and curled her body around it, not wanting the light to bother anyone.

"Is that a night light?" whispered Charity.

Sena braced herself for the inevitable mockery she knew was coming. She was surprised when instead of making fun of her Charity asked, "Can you put it in the middle?"

Sena rolled over and put the light in the darkness

between them. Tiny specks of light reflected in the tears on Charity's cheeks. "Thanks," she whispered, and the two girls stared at the little light until the motions of the ship rocked them to sleep.

Sena awoke the next morning to find the cabin empty, and sunlight streaming in through the open balcony door. She went outside and found Charity sitting in one of the chairs, wearing jeans and a long-sleeved sweater, staring out over the water.

"Where are Ted and Claire?" asked Sena, blinking in the bright light.

"They went to get breakfast, and they're bringing some back for us."

"That was nice of them."

"Did you know their son died last year?"

Sena nodded. "Yeah, Claire mentioned it. Do you know what happened?"

"He was hit by a car, riding his bike home from school."

"Wow, that really sucks."

"You never know what's going to happen. Everything can change so fast."

"Are you okay?" Sena asked. "You don't seem like yourself very much."

Charity blurted, "If we get out of this I'm going to try to be a better person. I am going to be a good daughter, and I'm going to sell my stuff and give the money to the poor. I don't care about being popular or having the best clothes anymore."

Sena looked at Charity curiously. "You're going to give away all your stuff?"

"Yep."

"And stop being popular?"

"Maybe."

"How's that going to make you a better person?"

Charity thought about it. "I don't know. Maybe it won't. I feel like I need to do something different, or be a different way."

"Do you want a suggestion?" Sena asked, feeling like she was walking on thin ice.

"Sure."

"It's not about your clothes or popularity. It's about how you act and make other people feel. You could keep all of your clothes and just be nicer to people. That would make you a better person."

Charity was silent, looking down at her bare feet. Sena noticed her toenails were turquoise blue, and one nail on each foot was painted like a tiny cupcake.

"I think I owe you an apology," said Charity, so quietly Sena almost missed it.

"What? No, we're fine. You don't owe me an apology."

"Yes I do," insisted Charity. "I've been a huge jerk to you and I'm sorry."

Sena hoped Charity was serious about being nicer. At least she was trying.

"Did you see that?" Charity asked, shading her eyes and looking out at the water.

"No," said Sena, relieved by the change of subject.

"I think it was a dolphin. Look, another one!" Charity's face was lit by the biggest smile Sena had ever seen on her. "I love dolphins. I'm going to be a marine biologist someday. Have you ever been swimming with dolphins?" She didn't wait for an answer. "I've always wanted to, but I don't think wild dolphins should be captured for tourist attractions. Someday maybe I'll get to though. Aren't they beautiful?"

There were a lot of dolphins now, leaping in graceful arcs around the ship. Sena looked at Charity; her face was radiant with joy.

Her expression changed suddenly to a look of disgust. Sena turned in time to see a red bag sail down and land in the water.

"You're a sick jerk!" shouted Charity to the offensive, out-of-sight passenger.

And with that, the moment was broken.

CHAPTER NINE

AFTER BREAKFAST, THE GIRLS decided to look for their classmates. To Sena, the passengers seemed less optimistic and more resigned. Instead of conversations and singing, she saw people sitting on their mattresses or pool chairs looking lost and staring into space. All they could do was wait and worry about their families back home and their own fates.

They walked past one woman sitting on the stairs, sobbing for her children. Several people sat near her, offering comfort. Her weeping followed Sena and Charity long after they had left her far behind.

Sena picked up a snippet of conversation between two male crew members as they passed.

"Did Brady ever show up for his shift this morning?"

"I don't think so. He's probably off somewhere enjoying the perks of his new job."

Their coarse laughter faded as they turned a corner.

When Sena and Charity finally found their class at the distant end of the Lido deck, they discovered the students were in the middle of a lecture by Mr. Stoddard about cargo ships.

"Container ships are the big rigs of the sea. Each one has stacks and stacks of truck-sized containers piled as high as a small building. They look like floating apartment blocks. The containers can hold all kinds of things, and they're very efficient. Here's a bit of trivia I think is interesting. Did you know it it's cheaper to catch fish in Scotland, freeze it, ship it to China on a container ship, thaw it and let the Chinese filet it, freeze it again and ship it back to Scotland, rather than to have the Scots filet it themselves?

"It's going to be important that these container ships keep operating until we can get the country back on its feet. Without them, there will be all kinds of shortages – especially food shortages."

"How many containers are filled with food usually?" asked one student.

"I don't know, you'd have to see the ship's manifest, but not even the captain of a container ship gets to see the manifest."

"What's a manifest?" asked Sena.

"It's a list of all of the goods being transported on a ship. Most ships don't have any idea what they're carrying, unless it's flammable or dangerous. They don't always declare that either. A few years ago a news team wanted to make a point about the lack of oversight in the shipping industry and they actually shipped a container of spent uranium to Los Angeles."

"Isn't that the stuff they make bombs out of?"

"Yes, and run nuclear reactors. Of course, after 9/11, security was improved, but shipping is still probably the biggest industry that no one knows anything about. Do you guys think you own anything that was ever on a transport ship?"

The students looked at themselves and at each other.

"Maybe our phones?" asked someone.

"Yes. What else?"

"Our clothes?"

"What about back home? How many things in your houses got there via container ship?"

The class was silent, thinking of their homes and families. Sena heard a few sniffles, and thought to herself that Mr. Stoddard's lecture probably wasn't having the intended effect.

"Would you be surprised if I told you almost everything in your homes, at your jobs, and in the classroom came to the U.S. on a boat like that? Ninety percent of all goods in the world are shipped on container boats."

Charity rolled her eyes. "Not my Ray-Bans. They were made in Italy."

Sena was kind of glad that Charity was back to normal.

"As nice as it is to imagine your designer sunglasses flying first class from Italy and enjoying the in-flight movie, most Ray-Bans are made in China and cross the ocean on a slow-moving boat piled high with boxes."

"What-*ev*-er," said Charity under her breath. "Do you guys want to get out of here?"

Sena looked around and realized Charity was including her. Maybe she wasn't completely back to normal.

"Come on," she whispered, and moved slowly away from the lecture and into the crowd of passengers. They regrouped at the buffet and Sena stepped in something slippery.

"Ew," she said, stepping back. Rivulets of cooking oil and grease flowed from the shutdown hamburger bar and across the deck. She got out her camera and took a picture.

A woman in a crumpled house dress and floppy hat

said, "The boat is listing so much, the grease spilled out of the fryers." She wrinkled her nose. "I hope they get it cleaned up by lunch time, it really stinks."

Sena didn't see anyone dealing with it, and figured the crew wasn't going to keep doing all the menial tasks onboard for much longer. They probably weren't going to get paid for this trip, so there wasn't any compelling reason for them to spend the morning cleaning up someone else's greasy mess.

She saw an Asian man in a white crew uniform arrive with a cleaning cart. She tried to tell him thanks but he refused to meet her eyes. She took a photo of him as he scrubbed to document how hardworking the crew was through the ordeal.

"What do you guys want to do?" Charity said. Sena moved to rejoin the group.

Jessica said, "I heard there's bingo this morning."

"Tell me you did not just suggest we play bingo with the old folks." Charity rolled her eyes.

"Have you ever tried it? They are like striking cobras with those stampers."

"I don't think I even want to know what you're talking about," said Charity. "Come on, who else has an idea? Something inside, it's freezing up here."

Sena looked at the sky and saw a mass of gray clouds on the northern horizon. She hoped it wasn't heading towards them. The thought of cold rain soaking all of the mattresses and bedding on deck made her shiver.

Spending another afternoon in the library sounded like fun to her, though she wasn't about to suggest it. She was still trying to take in the fact she'd been invited to join Charity's circle and didn't want to risk spoiling it.

"Did you have something in mind?" That was Kade.

"I was thinking we could go exploring," Sena suggested.

"Like where? Maybe the crew only area? I've got a keycard," said Paris. "I was flirting with one of the cabin boys and he gave it to me along with directions to his room." She rolled her eyes. "As *if*."

"Do you want to see something creepy?" Charity said. "I heard there's a morgue on the ship."

"I'm sure that's off-limits," Kade said.

"Exactly," said Charity. "It's perfect. Who's in?"

Sena reached into her pocket for her book light. When she touched it, she said, "I'm in, and I know where it is."

The stairs were still lit by glow sticks, so they weren't too dark. At the bottom, they found the crew door and Paris opened it with her keycard. Sena had half hoped the batteries in the lock would be dead, but the green light blinked on with a cheerful chirp, and they pushed the door open. The hallway loomed in front of them like a gaping black maw, and Sena flicked on her little light.

Everyone spoke in whispers, despite the fact that the area looked deserted except for them. A few of the kids had mini flashlights on their keychains, and they led the way, tiny beams of light slicing into the darkness.

Jessica screamed, and Sena about jumped out of her skin, while one of the guys laughed. "Got ya," he said to Jessica.

"I'm going to kill you!" she said, laughing too.

The bumpy rubber flooring beneath Sena's feet reminded her how the stainless steel had looked in full light, stretching endlessly ahead of her. She tried to remember which door led to the morgue. The teens passed several doors until they came to the area with the walk-in freezers.

"Check this out," one of the guys said. He motioned for them to follow him into one of the smaller freezers. It was barely cooler inside than in the hallway.

"What is it?" asked Charity.

"Heaven," he said. Flashlights revealed shelves and shelves of ice cream. It dripped from cardboard boxes, forming sticky puddles on the ground.

"More like hell. It's all melted."

They looked around the freezer, hoping to find one last carton that was still frozen.

Kade found a container of whipped topping and opened it. He glanced over at Charity, and then scooped out some of the fluff onto his finger and held it to Sena.

She wasn't sure what she was supposed to do.

"It's okay, try it," he said.

She hesitated and then licked a tiny bit from his finger. It was rich and sweet.

Kade traced her lips with the rest of the whipped cream on his finger. She opened her mouth slightly, wanting more. In the darkness she felt him lean toward her and thought he was about to kiss her. She'd never been kissed, and she closed her eyes in anxious expectation.

A loud crash startled them apart, and Sena looked over to see Charity staring at them. Next to Charity, one of the guys stood up from where he'd fallen. He held out a container and said sheepishly, "Sorry, I slipped. A guy's gotta have his Rocky Road."

"Come on, let's go find the morgue," Charity said in a clipped voice. "Which way, Sena?"

With reluctance and some relief, Sena stepped away from Kade and toward the door, the sweet taste of whipped cream on her lips.

Not far down the hallway, Sena was surprised to see a door standing ajar. She caught a whiff of a terrible, fishy smell and knew she'd found the seafood freezer.

As they approached, the smell of fish and other seafood beginning to decay was thick and cloying. Kids groaned and gagged and Sena wasn't sure if they were serious or faking. She pulled the neck of her t-shirt up over her nose and mouth to try to block some of the smell, and pointed to the door of the morgue.

Paris's keycard didn't work the first time, and Sena hoped they would all want to leave. Paris realized she had the card upside down, and on the second try, the green light blinked, the lock chirped, and they opened the door.

It was forbiddingly dark in the next room, and the air had a smoky tang to it. It wasn't bad, exactly. More ominous. She was sure the bodies of the people who'd been killed in the fire were inside and she didn't want to be there anymore, regardless of what Charity or her friends thought of her. She decided to wait out in the hallway.

She hoped Kade would want to wait out in the hallway with her, but he followed his friends into the morgue without so much as glancing at her.

Sena stood alone by the partially open door and tried to ignore the fishy smell. Instead she thought about what had almost happened in the ice cream freezer; Kade McGuire had been about to kiss her.

She touched her lips with her fingers and let herself imagine what it would have been like to feel his mouth on hers. She floated away in daydreams involving her and Kade and a field of daisies in the warm sunshine.

Then she heard a sound that snapped her back to reality. The lock at the far end of the hall chirped, signaling that someone had opened the door and was heading their way.

She stepped quickly into the morgue, trying to see through the gloom in the faint glow of her book light.

Someone jumped out from behind the door at her and grabbed her arm.

She stifled a scream and almost burst into tears. "That wasn't funny!" she said, nearly forgetting why she was there.

"Aw, I'm sorry. I wish I could've seen your face though. Talk about the right time and the right place," said the guy that liked Rocky Road ice cream.

"Be quiet," she hissed. "Someone's coming."

"Probably getting lunch supplies," said Charity quietly. "They won't come in here."

"We should still hide," said Sena. "Do you know how much trouble we'll be in if we're caught?" The thought of being caught breaking the rules made her stomach clench tightly.

It was too dark for Sena to tell if Charity shrugged or rolled her eyes; she suspected both.

"Fine," Charity said. "We'll hide. Come on guys, behind the counter."

In the back of the room was a long, low counter that acted as a divider between the morgue shelves and a large desk. It probably wasn't much of a hiding place with the lights on, but in the complete dark Sena hoped it would be enough if someone came in.

The whispers and giggles quieted immediately when they all heard voices outside the door of the morgue, and then the quick beep as the door was unlocked. Sena flicked off her light and willed herself to breathe silently. Being discovered would be worse than being in the dark for a few minutes, she tried to convince herself.

She couldn't make out the low-spoken male voices because her heart was pounding in her ears and practically out of her chest. Why had she come along with Charity? She should be reading in the library or watching the sea for dolphins. If they were caught in here, the captain would probably put them in the brig for breaking and entering.

Sena tried to calm down so she could hear what was being said. When her brain finally sorted out what she was hearing she was dizzy with real fear.

The voices were speaking Korean.

She tried to listen but could only pick out a few words, and none of them made any sense.

Why were the Koreans in here? They moved some of the rolling morgue shelves around, and then spoke quietly about… a plan?

Their voices were frustratingly soft. They only spoke for a few minutes and then they left.

The high schoolers remained hidden behind the low counter, making sure they were really gone. Finally, Kade stood and whispered, "I don't know what they were saying, but it didn't sound friendly."

A few of the others murmured their agreement. Sena turned her light back on and looked around to try and figure out why the men had chosen the morgue for their covert meeting. Maybe something to do with the morgue shelves.

Instead of having body drawers like the morgues she'd seen on TV, the ship's morgue had shelves on one side of the room with pull-out pans for bodies. She was sorry to see so many silver body bags on the shelves. A lot of people had died on the cruise so far. She'd known about the ones in the fire, but that didn't account for the number of body bags she saw now.

Then she noticed that one of the bodies wasn't in a bag.

"Was that here earlier?" she asked Charity, pointing at the body.

"No," said Charity. "Hey, shine your light over there, would you?"

The Rocky Road guy pointed his flashlight at the body. It was wearing a crew uniform, and it wasn't burned.

"Holy crap," said someone. Sena took a step forward and felt sick when she thought she recognized the body.

The drawer pulled out with a creak and one of the girls screamed. Sena wanted to scream, but couldn't. Her mouth had gone completely dry with fear.

The body on the shelf belonged to Captain Brady.

CHAPTER TEN

"IS HE REALLY DEAD?" asked Jessica.

Paris made an exasperated noise. "Duh. Look at his throat. We've got to tell someone."

"Good one, brainiac," said Charity. "Let's go find Captain Crane."

"Wait," said Sena.

"Now what?" asked Charity.

"What if he's in on it?"

"Captain Crane? Come on."

"No really," said Sena. "Captain Brady was going to get Crane in trouble for abandoning the ship."

"Hmm," said Charity, thinking aloud. "And he's the one that brought the Koreans onboard in the first place, right?"

"That's what I'm thinking," said Sena. "He's not even next in line for captain."

"Who is then?"

"I don't know. Maybe Chief Huang, the head of Engineering? I really have no idea."

"Then who do we tell?" asked Jessica. Her voice had taken on a new shrillness, and Sena thought she was close to panic.

"Let's go up to the bridge and see who's in charge."

The wind outside was icy after the warmer, stuffy air

below decks. Any hope Sena had that the storm was going to bypass them was dashed when she came out of the stairwell and saw angry gray clouds thick overhead. The motion of the ship underfoot was more noticeable as well. The surf was getting rougher.

After they pounded on the crew-door leading to the bridge, it opened and an officer Sena didn't recognize glared at them.

"We need to talk to whoever's in charge," said Charity.

"The captain doesn't have time to chit-chat with a bunch of kids."

"The captain?" said Kade. "Captain Brady's here?"

"Captain Crane."

"What about Captain Brady?" blurted out Jessica.

"What about him?" said the crewman with a sneer. "He hasn't bothered showing up for duty since yesterday afternoon. Probably drunk off his gourd below deck. He was insubordinate anyway. Good riddance."

"Can we talk to Captain Crane?" Jessica asked, close to tears.

"What's the problem? Rich girl can't take a hot shower and wants to complain straight to the captain? I don't think so. You kids beat it."

"But Captain Brady is—ow!" Jessica yelped when Charity pinched her arm.

"Never mind her. You're right, she just needs a shower. Come on, Jess," said Charity, starting to lead the girl away.

"No, we need to tell him," said Sena.

"I thought you said he might be in on it," Charity hissed.

"What if he's not?" said Sena. "If he is, then he already knows. If he's not, more people could die."

"What's going on out here?" came a voice Sena recognized as Crane's.

"I was telling these kids to get lost," said the officer.

Crane began to turn away when Sena said loudly, "We know where Captain Brady is." She studied Crane's face carefully, searching to see if he would betray any guilt. The only emotion she could read was annoyance.

"*Staff* Captain Brady was relieved of his responsibilities when he didn't show up for duty."

Sena had an inappropriate urge to giggle at the word 'duty.'

"He didn't show up because he's dead," blurted Jessica.

Crane narrowed his eyes. "I doubt that. Probably had too much to drink. It happens to the best of us."

"He's not drunk," said Sena. "He's dead. He was killed by the Koreans *you* brought back onboard."

"What?" said Crane incredulously. "Where?" They told him, and he turned to the crewman. "Go check it out."

The captain invited them to join him on the bridge while they waited for the sailor to return, and Sena hoped they weren't walking into a trap.

Instead of the debauchery and recklessness Sena halfway expected, she saw maps and charts strewn around the room on tables and pinned to walls. There were lists of passengers with young children or special needs, next to figures showing the total number of people aboard and how many passengers and crew were assigned to each lifeboat.

Lydia stood in front of one of the lists with a pencil in hand, writing out the names of casualties and causes of death and discussing it with the actress.

Mona, thought Sena, remembering she was the captain's girlfriend. She saw that although the original twenty names had fire or smoke inhalation as the cause of death, another ten or so names had been added. Had the Koreans killed them too?

No, the causes of death weren't violent. Heart attacks caused by failed pacemakers and stress were predominant, though she saw one victim had died of head injuries after a fall down the stairs.

"Did everyone with a pacemaker die?" Sena asked.

"No, only those heavily dependent on them," said Lydia.

"What is all this?" Kade asked the captain.

"We're going to use the lifeboats to get everyone back home," said Crane, "and we need to modify the muster assignments a bit, to make sure everyone gets a seat on a boat. We have life rafts to supplement the lifeboats, but they aren't properly stocked and I'm not sure they're navigable to Seattle. It's better to have every lifeboat full. We know we're on our own, so we need to get it right the first time."

"How do we know you aren't going to bail on us again?" said Kade.

Sena gawked at the rudeness of it. Crane just sighed. "I don't blame you for asking. There's no excuse for what I did, and I will always regret it. My goal now is to get everyone safely ashore."

He paused. "Now what's this about Brady? Tell me exactly what happened and what our guests have to do with it."

Before they could tell him, the deck trembled slightly and then lurched beneath their feet. Everyone staggered and tried to keep from falling, while a low moaning sound echoed around them.

"What the..." began Kade, and the captain spoke loudly to his crew.

"That was an explosion! Get down to engineering and see what's going on!"

Before the men could respond to the order, a bright light flashed in the bridge followed moments later by a loud crack and a roar. The deck pitched and bucked beneath them and they all lost their footing. Tables tipped and maps and glasses fell to the deck in a tinkle of broken shards.

Sena was on her hands and knees on the floor, a loud sound of nothing in her ears. She saw Jessica screaming, the sound muffled, while blood dripped from her hands. Sena shook her head to clear it, and tried to stand. Her legs were wobbly, but the movement of the deck had slowed and she regained her footing.

The captain was also standing. His eyes were so wide Sena could see the whites all the way around.

The crewman he'd sent below to check the morgue burst into the room and shouted, "Fire below deck and on the Lido! The whole thing blew up!"

Mona rushed to the captain's side. "Let's go, love. We can take the boat again, it's still below."

Captain Crane put his hands on her face, one on each cheek and looked tenderly into her eyes. "Not this time, *querida*. I abandoned my ship once. I won't make that mistake again."

"What about me?" Mona's voice was a whine.

"You go. I will come when I can." He straightened his shoulders and then said loudly, "I will not fail my ship again."

His tone was so dynamic and comforting, Sena took

an inadvertent step towards him, then she realized her center of gravity had changed. The ship's list had grown more noticeable and she put her arms out to keep her balance.

"You kids, get to a lifeboat!"

"Which one?" asked Kade, glancing at the carefully thought out evacuation plans.

"Go," said Captain Crane. "There's no time. Find one with room and get on. Hurry!" He turned to his crew. "We must abandon ship. Get the passengers to safety and do your duties like men!"

Sena could hardly believe it was the same man who had abandoned them on the first day. He'd been given a second chance and it was obvious he intended to make good on it.

Before Sena could attempt another step, Charity grabbed her hand and together with their classmates they fled the bridge.

Outside, the air was filled with smoke and screams. People were terrified by the explosions and the increasing tilt of the deck below their feet.

The students reached the first muster station and saw it was mobbed with people trying to push their way forward to the stepladder to board the lifeboat. A pretty young girl Sena recognized from the buffet line stood at the top and tried to tell people to form a line, however, no one listened. They all shuffled and wedged shoulders or feet ahead of the each other, trying to squeeze forward without blatantly cutting in line.

Several crew members were already on the boat, tugging on ropes and checking pulleys, getting the craft ready to launch, while a few sat and watched. Sena realized they weren't there to help, they were just making sure they got a seat.

She saw a mother trying to put an adult sized life-jacket on a baby. Her hands trembled too violently to snap the belt.

An elderly woman pushed a man in a wheelchair, begging for someone to help her get her husband off the boat.

The scariest sight of all was the orange glow coming from behind them near the middle of the ship. The ship was on fire again, and this time they weren't going to be able to put it out.

They had to get off.

The students tried to find a lifeboat with available space, but every muster station was swarming with what looked like more people than the lifeboats could hold.

They were on the starboard side of the ship, which was the side riding higher in the water. It was becoming harder to stand up straight, especially with the clutter and confusion of mattresses, pillows and bedding at every muster station. They leaned against the wall of the ship, and tried to decide where to go.

The angle of the ship made it difficult to launch the lifeboats, and two sailors were attempting to lower a full boat to the water. It dangled more than four stories above the open water, held up by a system that didn't look like more than a couple of pulleys and ropes.

The back end of the boat dropped a few feet and everyone inside screamed. The sailors yelled back and forth at each other, trying to figure out how to lower the boat. The back end dropped again and hung at a sickening angle. Sena wanted to close her eyes or turn away. Wasn't the crew trained on how to launch a lifeboat?

She pushed up her glasses and looked more closely at the men trying to lower the boat. She recognized one and after a moment of trying to place him realized he was the librarian. Why was a librarian trying to launch a lifeboat? And, she realized, *he* was the one who knew how to work the ropes and pulleys. It was the other crewman that was making it worse.

The people in the lifeboat were going to die if the sailors didn't get their act together right away. She held her breath when a sailor leaped from the railing of the ship to the roof of the lifeboat.

She gasped when she saw it was Danny. He took over for the incompetent sailor and grabbed the ropes. He shouted something at the librarian, and they worked together to straighten the lifeboat.

Sena wanted to cheer for him as the boat was lowered a bit at a time until they released it to drop the final few feet to the water. The scream of the passengers was audible, but turned to a cry of relief when they splashed safely into the water.

Sena was glad Danny was off the ship. That was, until she saw him climbing back up the rope. He swung over the railing and leaned down to catch his breath, hands on his knees. He straightened and looked straight into her eyes. "Oh no," he said, dismayed. "You're not supposed to be here. Why aren't you on your lifeboat?"

"It's gone, remember?"

As the words came out of her mouth, Sena realized it wasn't gone at all. It just wasn't at the muster station. "I totally forgot! It's tied to the other side of the ship." She practically danced with excitement. There was a boat for them after all.

"Go on then, get somewhere safe."

"What about you?"

Danny glanced around and she followed his eyes. Another lifeboat hovered in the air, its crew struggling to launch it.

"It's not their fault, you know," said Danny. He pointed at one of the men. "That guy runs the gift shop and the other one's a dishwasher. They were never trained in this. I've got to go help them."

"How come you know how to do it?" she called after him.

He paused and turned back, a grin lighting his face. "You know me and ship duties." Then he was running toward the lifeboat.

Sena pushed off the wall and called to her classmates, "We've got to get to the other side!"

Not waiting to see if they'd follow, she ran awkwardly toward the doors leading to the lounge. She fought gravity to try to open them, but they were too heavy. Kade and another student braced themselves and gave a count before pulling together. With great effort, they got the door open and hurried inside.

It wasn't completely dark; there were some windows and skylights in the lounge, and when Sena's eyes adjusted she started to run. Then she stopped. There were people in the room, sitting on couches and at tables. Why weren't they trying to get away?

"Abandon ship!" Kade shouted. "Follow us, we have a lifeboat!"

No one moved, and Sena realized they must be in shock. They were in a black zone and wouldn't move, even when she tugged an arm. They had been through too much, and now they'd shut down completely.

Out of the entire room, only one woman stood and

followed Kade, a blank look on her face and a baby in her arms.

Sena pulled at an elderly woman's arm until she shook her off.

"It's no use," said Kade. "They won't listen."

It was much easier to open the port side door back to the muster stations, and Sena saw that the crowds of people were thinning considerably as lifeboats launched successfully and carried them away.

"Over there," she pointed at the rail. It was the top of the pilot ladder, leading down to where Captain Crane had moored their lifeboat when he came back aboard.

The port side of the ship was lower in the water, and it gave Sena a feeling of vertigo to look over the side. It felt like she might topple right over the railing and into the sea.

How were they going to be able to climb down a ladder if they were falling away from it? She didn't think she had the arm strength to do it.

She saw the top of a man's head as he descended the ladder. His feet slipped off the rungs and he dangled from the ladder by his hands. Sena caught her breath. She yelled down something encouraging to the man and after he found his footing he glanced up at them.

It was one of the Koreans, and he was wearing a crew uniform instead of the blue jumper. At the sight of it she cursed herself. It was the same man she'd seen cleaning up the mess at the hamburger bar earlier. How could she not have noticed? He must have had more than cleaning supplies on his cart. He'd probably rigged some kind of explosion. There were a lot of cleaners and fuel onboard, and it could probably be done if you knew how. She just wished she knew why.

He'd almost reached the bottom of the ladder, and he hung by his arms for a moment before landing squarely on the fiberglass roof of the lifeboat. He moved quickly to the door and reached inside. When he stood up again he was holding something that struck fear all the way to her core.

A gun — a long, heavy automatic weapon.

He pointed it up at the ship and fired a volley at the people along the railing. They screamed and threw themselves to the deck. Dizzy with terror, Sena heard bullets ping into the metal railing.

The assault on the cruise ship stopped when he turned to face the other lifeboats bobbing in the water. She realized what he was about to do and another scream tore from her throat. The bitter wind caught the sound and carried it out to sea where it mixed with the screams of the helpless victims in the lifeboats.

It was a shooting gallery.

Sena looked again at the gunman. Though he was some distance away, she could see his face clearly. For the first time she saw an expression other than careful blankness or hidden contempt.

The man was laughing.

CHAPTER ELEVEN

ONE BY ONE, THE lifeboats that had already been launched began to move away from the threat as they turned on their engines and fled. The Korean pointed at them and yelled a command. His lifeboat moved to follow them in a macabre, slow-motion hunt. Sena hoped the sea was too choppy for him to aim or catch up with them.

The last lifeboat was almost finished loading, and they shouted for the high school kids to hurry. Sena stood to run to the boat, then noticed Charity slumped on the deck.

"Come on, get up, we've got to go!" she said, shaking her shoulder.

Charity groaned and raised her head, and Sena noticed that her shirt was soaked with blood. "Charity, oh no! What happened?"

"The gun, I think. I don't know." She looked at herself and then back up at Sena. "You should go, or they're going to leave."

"What?" asked Sena. Then she realized the others were running towards the boat. "I'm not going to leave you."

"You have to go. It's the last boat."

Sena ignored her. "Can you stand?" She put Charity's arm around her neck and tried to help her up.

"Ow ow, stop!" cried Charity. "Are you trying to kill me? I'll be fine. I think I might pass out anyway…"

Sure enough, Charity's head lolled to the side and she went limp in Sena's arms.

Sena looked toward the lifeboat again. Her classmates were almost to the stepladder which would take them onto the boat. She saw Kade get to the ladder and help Jessica and Paris aboard, followed by the woman with the baby. Rocky Road ice cream guy (she should have found out his real name) went up next.

Charity was unconscious but still breathing.

"Charity! Sena!" She looked up at the sound of her name. Kade shouted at her and waved for her to come.

She shook her head with exaggerated movement and gestured that he should go ahead. He put a hand on the rung of the ladder and she thought he would go too, but he spoke to the crew member and turned to point at them. The sailor shook his head and shrugged, then climbed aboard.

Kade ran back to her, jumping and tripping over discarded luggage and bedding, and shouting when he got close. "You have to come. They're leaving right now!" He skidded to a halt when he saw that Charity was hurt. He looked from her to Sena and quickly took in the situation. "I'll carry her."

He leaned over and gently took Charity in his arms, then tried to stand. The angle of the deck under his feet made it hard to get his balance and he stumbled.

"Okay, let's go," he said after Sena helped steady him, and tried to run. The awkwardness of the deck, along with Charity's weight made it impossible.

Sena looked at the lifeboat and saw it was already being lowered to the water.

They weren't going to make it.

Kade saw their chance of escape disappearing and a half-sob escaped his lips. "I told them to wait!" He took a few more steps forward, but it was too late, and they both knew it. Sena saw defeat on his face and in every line of his body. He carefully set Charity down on a mattress and Sena found a blanket to press to her wound and try to slow the bleeding. It was a useless gesture, she knew.

Kade straightened. "I'm going to go see if there are any boats left on the other side."

Sena nodded, and when he hurried away, she was not sure if she'd ever see him again.

She smoothed the hair back from Charity's face and sang her a lullaby while the water slowly rose higher. The sun was almost down, and the coming storm brought a cold wind, making the water choppy and gray.

Except for the wind and the groaning of the ship, it had grown quiet, almost peaceful, and she wondered how many people were still alive on the enormous vessel. Soon, it would be over for all of them.

She tried not to think of slipping beneath the waves into the darkness below. Instead, she thought of her mom. She hoped she was safe somewhere, either being cared for in the women's prison, or released.

In the letters they'd written back and forth they made plans to get a little house together when she was released. Her mom promised she'd make up for all the years she'd screwed up. They'd learn to garden and grow flowers, and there would be a whole room full of shelves and shelves of books for Sena.

"Sena!"

She turned at her name, expecting to see Kade, but it was Ted and Claire, the couple who had shared their room with her. Claire was pale and walked with a limp while Ted supported her. Their clothing was singed and their faces were splotchy with soot.

They scanned the deck looking for lifeboats as they came toward her, and Sena saw Claire's body sag.

"They're gone, they're all gone," whispered Claire, before turning on her husband in anger. "You should have left without me! Now we're both going to die and Maddie won't have anyone. Do you have any idea what that will do to her?"

"Settle down, Claire, we're not going to die."

"She'll never know what happened to us. She's going to need us, Ted, and we won't be there. We failed Jacob and now we've failed Dee." Claire covered her face and sunk to her knees. "Oh, my children."

Sena looked away, an awkward witness to Claire's raw pain.

"Claire. *Claire!* Snap out of it. We're not dead yet." Ted shook her by the shoulders. "Look, see those barrels? Those are life rafts. They're our ticket out of here."

Sena followed his finger and saw a large white cylinder mounted at the railing of the ship atop a square bin. Ted was studying the safety poster nearby when Kade burst out of the lounge, followed by Danny. Lydia and Captain Crane followed close behind.

"Let me give you a hand with that," said Danny to Ted, removing the railing around the contraption and adroitly unlocking the mechanism that secured it to the ship.

"Now we're going to heave the whole thing over. On my count. One, two, three!"

Danny and Kade pushed an orange billowy cube overboard, connected to the white cylinder. The cube unrolled like a giant slinky made of parachute fabric, stretching down to the water.

At the bottom of the slide-chute, a black and orange life raft popped out of the barrel and immediately began to self-inflate, unfolding and puffing up until there was a small life raft bobbing in the rough sea below them, tethered to the slide and the ship.

"Is that safe?" asked Claire, looking dubiously into the entrance to the escape chute.

"Safer than here," said Ted.

"Remove your heels," said Danny, pointing at Lydia's pumps. Everyone else was wearing flip flops or sneakers and Danny said they could keep their shoes on.

They were on deck four, and although the cruise ship was lower in the water than it should be, they were still over two stories above sea level.

The captain approached, awkwardly carrying Charity. He looked at Ted and indicated the slide. "You go first and help everyone as they land."

Ted nodded and gave his wife's hand a squeeze before jumping into the blackness at the top of the chute.

"You next," the captain said to Claire, who limped barefoot to the opening and then slid inside. "Lydia," he said, "can you go with this girl and make sure she doesn't get stuck?"

"I want to take her," said Kade.

Lydia nodded, and went ahead, saying she'd help him when they reached the bottom.

Kade sat at the top of the slide, while the captain placed Charity in front of him. He wrapped his arms around the limp girl and then wriggled forward until they dropped out of sight.

Sena looked at the opening of the chute. It looked like

a hole leading over the side of the ship and into dark, black nothingness. She tried to step forward but her feet were riveted to the deck. She heard a crackling sound and looked up to see the orange glow of the fire where it burned on the upper decks. The explosion earlier must have torn a hole in the bottom of the ship, and she wondered whether the ship would sink first, or burn down to where she was. Waiting seemed far easier and safer than forcing her feet to take her forward into the night.

Captain Crane and Danny were talking, and she heard Danny say, "And then you're coming after me, right?"

"Not while there are people aboard."

"But Captain—"

"No. I made that mistake once, and hated myself for it. I won't do it again."

"Then I'll stay, I'll help you."

"You're a good boy, Danny, and you have to go now, that's an order. When your dad passed on I promised him I'd take care of you. Don't make a liar out of me. Crew the life raft and get everyone away from here."

"But —"

"There's more life left for you, son. Your dad would be so proud of you."

The captain embraced Danny, and stepped away.

"Do you know how to release the raft?" asked Captain Crane.

"Yes, sir," said Danny. He stepped back and gave a salute. Sena didn't think she'd seen any saluting on the ship until now. It felt right.

"Let's go," said Danny, not turning to see the captain go back to his ship. Sena knew they wouldn't see him again.

Danny took two steps forward and stopped when he realized Sena hadn't moved.

"What's wrong?" he said. "Are you scared of heights?"

"The dark," she whispered.

She thought he'd try to drag her to the opening or talk her into it. Instead, he stood and rubbed his chin thoughtfully, studying her. Then he leaned toward her, and brought his lips to a small piece of plastic on the front of her life jacket. She giggled nervously.

When he moved back, a tiny light twinkled on the front of her vest.

"How did you do that?"

"Water activated light," he said. "Now, no more stalling, it's time to go. I'll be right behind you."

Sena let him guide her to a sitting position at the top of the chute, and then she took a deep breath and held it. He gave her a push and she was falling, down, down into nothingness.

Inside, the chute was a tight spiral and she followed the curve of it around and around as she fell. The sides of the slide were slippery and wrapped closely about her. She made steady progress until she came to a sudden stop.

The nylon material tangled at her feet and she couldn't pass through. She was stuck, about halfway to the raft. Sena kicked at the knot, trying to loosen it and free herself. It wouldn't budge.

The shadowy fabric pressed in around her. She flailed and writhed, but although the material gave under her touch, it held her in place. She thought she felt hot breath on her neck and the image of a man's face loomed before her.

Panic took over and she screamed. With her kicking and punching the fabric, it loosened, and with no warning she was falling again.

Sobs of relief shook her body when strong arms lifted her from the bottom of the chute and helped her to a place in the life raft. She huddled there and watched Danny climb out of the chute and then reach into a pocket on the life raft and pull out a safety knife. He cut the lines that connected them to the burning ship, and they were free.

The raft had a nylon roof, like a dome tent, and Sena unzipped a small window and looked behind them. Flames rose high into the night sky, and she was ashamed their brilliance was a comfort to her. Ted and Danny struggled to paddle the raft out of danger, while Sena fixed her eyes on the ship, watching as it burned.

CHAPTER TWELVE

THE PITCHING OF THE raft in the turbulent sea and her constant shivering made Sena miserable. She forced herself to look around the interior in the dismal light cast by a small overhead lamp and had the disturbing thought that they might as well be at sea in a children's birthday party bouncy house. The sides and floor were merely inflated rubber.

The only openings were in the canopy; the entrance and the small window she'd unzipped earlier. She closed the window to keep water out, but it poured in through the door each time a wave crashed against the raft.

The seven of them sat in gallons of seawater that swirled around their lower bodies. Ted had a plastic yellow scoop which he used to bail the water out as quickly as he could.

The motion of the raft riding up and down over the breaking waves was nothing like being on the cruise ship. Everyone except Charity clutched at the handholds around the perimeter to keep from being tossed around inside or worse, slipping through the entrance and out into the raging sea.

Lydia and Kade each braced themselves with one hand, and supported Charity with the other.

There was a terrible chemical smell in the air, like rubber and plastic. The smell, along with the constant motion, made Sena nauseous. She closed her eyes as a massive wave crashed over them, blasting water everywhere and collapsing the top of the raft.

She held her breath, thinking it might be her last, until the canopy popped back into place and they ascended another wave. It was so steep she felt herself sliding and tightened her grip.

How long could the raft handle the pounding of the waves before it popped like a balloon, leaving them scrambling in a sinking trap of rubber?

In the flickering shadows, Sena saw Danny let go of his handhold and slide across the raft to the other side, where he busied himself with something lashed to a tie-down that looked like a bundle of tarp and ropes.

They hovered at the top of a cresting wave for a moment before it fell out from beneath them, leaving them to fall with a sickening slap and squeal of rubber into a deep trough. Danny lost his balance and fell heavily onto Kade, then righted himself and crawled back to the entrance.

He grasped the equipment and, after checking to make sure it was attached outside the raft, threw it overboard.

"What was that?" she shouted.

"An anchor so we don't flip!" he shouted back.

Sena decided that wasn't even a little bit reassuring. The smell and motion were really getting to her and she was afraid she was going to vomit. The thought of throwing up in the raft and having it tossed around on everyone was almost too much for her, and she unzipped her tiny window again, hoping the fresh air would settle her stomach.

She wished she could see outside so she could

anticipate when to brace herself. It was like riding a roller-coaster in the dark. Her muscles ached from gripping her handholds so tightly, but she couldn't relax when she had no idea when the next wave would hit.

It was a long, cold, miserable night, and by the time the sea grew calmer and the orange fabric of the canopy began to glow with early morning light, Sena was exhausted. More than that though, she was cold. Though it was late June, the water temperature of the north Pacific probably wasn't over fifty degrees Fahrenheit, and she was soaked with it.

"We're too cold," said Claire, speaking for the first time since they boarded the raft.

"I'm cold too," said Lydia. "And I could really go for a cup of tea right now."

"No, I mean we're *too* cold. I don't want to alarm anyone, but if we can't get warm we aren't going to last long out here."

Sena didn't think people should say they didn't want to alarm you and then say something completely alarming.

"What do you mean we won't last?" asked Kade. He'd found another plastic bailer and was helping Danny toss water outside.

"If your core temperature drops more than a few degrees you'll get hypothermia. It means your body is losing heat faster than it can warm itself up. If it's allowed to go on, it can be fatal."

Sena glanced at Charity. Ted was holding her on his lap to keep her up out of the water and help her stay warm. Her chest rose and fell with the rapid breaths passing between her blue lips. Sena's heart clutched in her chest. They had to help her.

A small wave crested outside the entrance to the raft and spilled inside, flowing around their legs and feet. She was already so cold and wet, the new water didn't make much difference. Lydia probably couldn't feel anything with her bare feet, which must be numb by now.

If only there was something to sit on to get them up off the floor of the raft. She considered her life vest, but there was no way she was taking that off.

She leaned back and was surprised to realize she was still wearing her backpack. That would be perfect to sit on. She pulled it off, and then noticed everyone watching. "I wear it so much I forgot I had it on," she explained with a shrug and a half-smile.

Sena unzipped the pack and looked inside. Although most of her things were soaked a few were only damp. "I don't think the library is going to want these back," she said, handing two ruined books to Kade. "Maybe someone can sit on them."

She also had her school uniform, a couple of extra shirts, five pairs of socks and underwear, a swimsuit, and the real treasure — a fleece-lined windbreaker with a hood. "Here, put this around Charity," she said, passing the jacket to Ted.

The outer pocket of the backpack was full of the batteries Kade had given her, useless now since the book light had been ruined by the water. She fingered it sadly before putting it back in the pack.

She also had a pack of tissue (ruined), a deck of cards (probably ruined), and her laminated map of the ship (not ruined, but useless). Next she pulled out a pair of cheap binoculars. They'd been on the suggested packing list, and her foster father had let her bring an old pair he no longer used. She thought that might be it until she took one last glance in the pack. Her eyes widened. The list also suggested they bring a hat, scarf and gloves. She'd shoved all three items in the bottom of her pack and promptly forgotten about them.

She felt like she had struck gold.

They used the scarf to sponge up the water on the floor, and then Sena passed around the clothing. Pretty soon almost everyone had either socks or mittens on their hands. Lydia put the socks on her feet and Sena wore the hat.

They were still cold and wet, but the waves had calmed and they were slightly better off than they'd been a few minutes ago. More importantly, they were more optimistic. No longer having to sit in a cold puddle was a huge boost to morale.

"Do we have any idea where we're going?" asked Kade.

"We'll have to wait and see," said Danny. "We're at a place in the Pacific where two currents meet. One circles up to Alaska and the other moves south. It's hard to say which of them will pick us up."

"How do you know so much about sailing?" asked Lydia. "Wasn't this your first time out?"

"It was my first time on the *Duchess*, yes," said Danny. "I grew up on the water. My dad was a fishing boat captain and when he and my mom split up, he took me out with him when it was his turn to have me."

"Any chance he'll come looking for you?" asked Kade hopefully.

"No," said Danny, ending the conversation.

Sena changed the subject. "It doesn't look like a very good design for a life raft. There's no engine or good way to get around."

Danny cursed the terrorists under his breath. "If it wasn't for them, we probably could have gotten into a lifeboat. Even if we hadn't, someone would have been floating in the area and given us a tug. The regular lifeboats have small engines."

"What I want to know is what kind of life raft doesn't have any water?" asked Kade.

"Of course!" said Danny, hitting himself on the head with the palm of his hand. "There are supposed to be emergency supplies in here. Anyone see anything?"

Near the entrance there were several pockets with zippers. He opened one and pulled out an orange plastic case. When he removed the socks from his hands, Sena noticed his fingers shook. "Let's see what we've got here."

He named the items so everyone could hear. "Looks like about eight flares, some fishing gear, a flashlight, mirror, first aid kit, air pump and patch kit, and some food and water, maybe two to three days' worth."

"Anything else?" Claire asked.

Danny unzipped the next pocket over and took out a compact orange package wrapped in plastic. He studied it, then a huge grin split his face. "Jackpot! It says it's thermal gear." He ripped one of the packages open. Sena heard Claire catch her breath, and turned to see tears on her cheeks.

Claire wiped at the moisture with the back of her hand and smiled wryly. "I guess I really shouldn't cry out here. Wasting water."

"We're going to be okay," said Ted, patting Claire's shoulder awkwardly in the crowded raft.

Danny showed them what kind of thermal gear they had. "We've got hand warmers, space blankets, and a fashionable thermal coverall for each of us."

"That's really going to clash with my skin tone," said Charity, her voice slurred.

"You're awake!" Sena exclaimed.

"Let's get this on you," said Claire.

The thermal outfit was a baggy jumpsuit made out of waterproof polymer and cloth material with a reflective coating inside. They carefully helped Charity get the suit on right over her clothes. She kept her arms next to her body and let the sleeves dangle down empty. It even had a hood, which they pulled up over her hair.

Danny figured out how to open the canopy part-way, and eventually everyone changed into the thermal suits and spread out their wet clothes to dry in the sun. Sena tried not to laugh at the spectacle they made trying to get into their suits.

They were seamless at the bottom so they had to be pulled on like a sleeping bag. Since it was nearly impossible to stand up on the raft, they had to wriggle and squirm to get them on. Charity cracked a smile at the sight.

Sena knew Ted and Claire were worried about Charity by the loaded glances they kept giving each other over her head. She asked Danny if he'd trade her places so she could sit by her friend.

Her friend.

If someone had told her before the cruise she and Charity would become friends, she wouldn't have believed them.

Charity was pale, and despite the chill there was a sheen of perspiration on her face. Her breathing was quick and shallow, and she spoke in short phrases.

"I'm sorry I made you miss... the lifeboat. If it wasn't

for me… you wouldn't be here."

"Don't say that. Who knows what would have happened if I went with the other boat? Maybe you saved my life too." Sena saw skepticism on Charity's face and added, "Really. I wouldn't change a thing."

There was a long pause, then Charity said, "I wish I'd told my mom and dad… I loved them."

"You're going to tell them, because we're getting you home."

"You don't understand, Sena."

Kade's voice cracked, "I'll tell them." Charity closed her eyes and Sena stared at the endless ocean.

It was so unfair. Charity was supposed to be having fun on a fancy cruise ship, not shot and dying in a life raft.

Then a thought crossed her mind. If the EMP had never happened, Charity would probably still be making fun of her and ordering her around. Even if that was true, she'd take the old Charity back in a minute if she was whole and healthy. Anything was better than this.

A movement caught her eye and she squinted in the bright sun reflecting on the deep blue sea. Was it a fish? The silvery body sparkled and then vanished beneath the waves before she could make it out.

There it was again.

"Do you guys see something over there?" she pointed.

They turned to look.

"See?"

There were more now, and they were coming closer. Soon she realized they weren't fish. They were dolphins.

"Charity has to see this." She touched her leg through the thermal suit and shook her. "Hey sleepyhead, wake up."

Charity opened her eyes with obvious effort and stared blankly at Sena.

"Look," said Sena.

Charity's eyes widened when she saw the dolphins and she winced as she tried to sit up higher for a better view. They were jumping and leaping past the raft now, hundreds of them. The water was alive with their splashing and their sleek bodies.

"They're beautiful," whispered Charity.

Too soon, the last of the pod flashed by and faded in the distance. Charity sighed and began to sink back down when they heard a series of whistles and clicks. A dolphin had his head above the waves and was watching them from the water.

"He's saying hi," grinned Kade. Charity's face glowed with happiness.

The dolphin stayed with them, circling the raft and performing tricks. He was dark gray with light gray patches on his sides, and his chin and belly were creamy white. A dark stripe ran from his beak to each of his intelligent eyes.

He dove down and then soared straight up out of the water, then came back down with hardly a splash. He entertained them with his antics for a long time, before finally leaping away to rejoin his pod.

"Now you can say you've swum with dolphins," said Sena, turning to Charity. Her eyes were open and blank, and she was still, a slight smile on her lips.

Tears filled Sena's eyes and she blinked rapidly to keep them from falling. "She loved dolphins," she choked out, and then pulled her knees up to her chest and rested her forehead on them to hide her face. She stayed like that for a long time.

CHAPTER THIRTEEN

WATER.

THAT'S ALL SENA could think about. They had rationed the small cans of survival water, and they were each allowed two swallows every couple of hours. Every time it was her turn for a drink she fantasized about tilting the can up, and letting all of the cool liquid flow down her parched throat.

Her thirst was getting worse, and each time she stopped herself at two sips it was the hardest thing she'd ever done. She was afraid someday she wouldn't be able to stop.

She eyed the others, scrutinizing them as they took their turns. Was that three swallows? Were they taking more than their share? She had the smallest mouth of anyone on the raft—shouldn't she get an extra sip to compensate?

There'd be even less water if Charity were here.

She hated herself for the thought.

The evening Charity had died, they'd wrapped her body securely in the thermal suit. It bothered Sena to think of her bobbing around in the water, but they didn't have anything to weigh her down. Hopefully the suit would fill with water and carry the body down.

That had been a couple of weeks ago, and as far as Sena could tell, they weren't any closer to land.

114

Sometimes she wondered if they were moving at all.

They had more food than water, also rationed. Ted said if they ate a lot of food, their bodies would have to use their own moisture to digest it, so they were limited to a few bites each day.

Sena was hungry, however, the discomfort of her hunger was eclipsed by her thirst.

"It's so ironic," she said one day. "We're surrounded by water and dying of thirst."

"We're not dying," said Danny, ever the optimist.

"Have you ever heard the saying, 'Water, water everywhere, but not a drop to drink?'" asked Claire. "I bet whoever made it up was stranded on a life raft in the middle of the ocean."

"You're close," said Lydia. "It's actually a poem about a sailor. It's called 'The Rime of the Ancient Mariner.' Do you want to hear a bit of it?"

Sena loved hearing Lydia's accent, her rich voice like warm honey.

"Day after day, day after day
We stuck, nor breath nor motion;
As idle as a painted ship
Upon a painted ocean.

Water, water, everywhere,
And all the boards did shrink;
Water, water, everywhere,
Nor any drop to drink."

"How does it end?" asked Danny. "Do they find land?"

Danny knew better than to speak of rescue. They had

an unspoken agreement not to mention it. Planes didn't fly over and ships were never sighted. The sea was unimaginably vast and no one was looking for them.

"Not exactly. The rest of the crew dies, but the sailor had killed a bird, so he is doomed to go through life telling his tale."

"For killing a bird?" Sena asked. If a bird landed anywhere near her right now it wouldn't stand a chance. She looked around at the others and wondered if anyone else was hungry or thirsty enough to eat a bird. A raw bird.

Kade stared at the canopy of the raft, his face blank. She was worried about him. He had barely spoken since Charity died and spent most of his time in silent contemplation of the raft's canopy. The only time she saw a spark of life in him was when it was time for their food or water ration. After that he went back to staring.

The sea stretched endlessly in every direction, and as the days and weeks passed, Sena didn't blame him for checking out.

To pass the time, everyone but Kade played games like *I Spy* or *Twenty Questions*. One day Danny suggested, "How about we play *Two Truths and a Lie*?" He explained that each person would say two things about themselves that were true and one thing that was a lie. The others had to guess which was the lie.

"I'll go first," said Danny. "I have been ice fishing. I'm eighteen years old. I've never had a cavity."

"That one's easy," said Claire. "You're not eighteen. That's the lie. I looked it up once, and you have to be twenty-one to get a job on a cruise ship."

The others looked to Lydia for confirmation and she nodded. "It's true."

"So is that your answer?" asked Danny. They nodded and he grinned. "Wrong! My dad knew the captain and he gave me a job as a favor to an old friend. I knew you'd guess that!"

"Where's your dad now?" Lydia asked.

Danny was silent a moment and then said, "With the captain."

Sena remembered the conversation she'd heard between Danny and the captain before she'd jumped into the chute and knew Danny's dad had passed away. She saw Lydia processing what Danny had said, and the moment realization hit her. She obviously felt bad for asking.

Danny saw Lydia's discomfort and gave her a small smile. "It's okay, I'm the one that brought it up. Let's keep going. Your turn."

Lydia said, "Three things. Right. I love horror movies. I'm scared of the dark. And I've got two dogs."

"Oh, I love horror movies too," said Claire. "Especially *Jaws*." She clapped a hand over her mouth. "I'm sorry, I didn't mean to say that!"

Merely the mention of sharks was enough to make Sena's heart beat faster. Twice the raft had shaken violently and they had seen a shark fin in the water. Ted sat closest to the door and he kept a paddle nearby to drive them off, but it was a toothpick compared to the huge sharks they'd seen.

Danny said they didn't need to worry about sharks, because the raft had two tubes that kept them afloat. If a shark bit a hole in one, the other would still be okay. What he left unsaid was that if they only had one tube, the raft would ride lower and fill with water again. Their suits wouldn't protect them from constant contact with

117

the icy cold sea. It would only be a matter of time before they died of hypothermia.

"How can you love horror movies and be afraid of the dark?" asked Ted, trying to take their minds off sharks. "People who are scared of the dark don't watch horror movies. I think one of those is the lie."

"She's not afraid of the dark," said Sena with certainty.

"Wait, have you ever heard her talk about dogs?" said Claire. "Don't you think she would have told us?"

"She's got a picture of something in that locket she's wearing," said Ted.

Danny sat closest to her and had seen the photos over her shoulder. "They're cute too."

"Oh, can we see?" asked Claire. Lydia passed around her locket for everyone to look at.

Claire studied it for several moments. "You're so lucky to have this. Her voice broke. "I'd give anything for a photo of my kids right now."

"Maybe we should play something else," Danny said. "This game is not turning out the way I thought it would."

"Hang on, let me try," said Sena. She decided to liven it up with outrageous statements.

"I once vomited in a child's eyes and blinded her."

"That's a real whopper," said Lydia.

"Were you seasick?" joked Danny.

"Okay, here's the second one—I had a tapeworm."

A chorus of "Ew," went up, and Danny added, "No wonder you're such a runt."

"Wait, are you saying one of those is true?" asked Claire, confusion wrinkling her brow.

"Last one," Sena said. "A meth lab exploded in my

kitchen."

"Wait, what?" said Danny.

An awkward silence fell.

Finally Lydia said in a hesitant voice, "Um, the tapeworm?"

Ted interrupted. "Okay, that's enough of that game. I think it's time for a drink."

Kade sat up. "I'm first."

After everyone had their sips of water the raft grew quiet as they prepared for sleep. On the second night Ted told everyone they would be warmer if they shared the thermal jumpers. Claire had tried to squeeze in with Ted, but it was impossible. He was too big to share with anyone.

Kade refused to share, which left Claire, Lydia, Sena and Danny. No one thought the two teens should share, though Sena and Danny both insisted they had no interest in any 'shenanigans,' as Lydia called it.

Claire offered to share with Sena, which left Lydia and Danny together. For the first hour or two Sena was uncomfortable about being so physically close to someone, and then the increased warmth changed her mind. Now sleeping near Claire was one of her few comforts. She snuggled up to Claire's back, and closed her eyes.

She hadn't thought about the meth lab in a long time. It was after Sena's grandmother had died, so Sena was living in her mother's apartment for the first time since she was a toddler. Sena's mother hadn't wanted to take her back but didn't want to give her away either, so she reluctantly made room for her daughter in the trashy, rundown apartment.

Ellisa Barr

Most of the house was off-limits to ten-year-old Sena, especially the kitchen. Then her mother forgot to feed her for two days in a row, and Sena decided to risk it.

Tubing, syringes and scissors were scattered among the various bottles and containers half full of chemicals, and lots of glassware. A heavy smell of cat pee hung in the air, though they didn't have a cat.

Tentatively she'd looked through the mess, trying to find something to eat, and that's how her mother had found her.

She was so angry.

Sena didn't know if it was out of worry for her child or because she thought she might ruin something in the lab, but that's when she started locking Sena in the closet.

Sena's eyes flew open and she tried to get enough moisture in her mouth to turn on the little light on her life jacket. When it was glowing, she sighed and rolled to her other side. Claire rolled too and put an arm around her, holding her close.

Not even her grandmother had held her like that. She was a very strict and formal woman, given more to cold silences and disapproving stares.

In the safety of Claire's arms, Sena dared close her eyes, and she was eleven years old again, back in her mom's apartment.

She'd learned a lot that summer. It was the summer she'd been introduced to her mom's new boyfriend, and the summer she'd started staying on the streets as much as possible in order to avoid him.

She learned that hotels had free breakfast every morning, and that the public library was open weekdays until nine. She discovered which parks had family

120

reunions on weekends and learned how to fill a plate with food and sneak away without drawing attention.

In short, she learned to survive.

Survival depended on a few simple rules and she was careful never to break her own code. Her most important rule was to remain unnoticed. This meant following rules and not causing conflict or making unnecessary eye contact. She had to act normal, inconspicuous, and never, ever look or smell like she lived on the street.

On Sunday mornings when the library was closed and her mom was sleeping off whatever bizarre cocktail she'd ingested the previous night, Sena went home to shower and do laundry and see if things had improved. They never had.

Today was Sunday so she would go home soon. First she was going to get some breakfast.

Sena approached the side door of the hotel and bent to untie her shoe. She was stalling. To get into the hotel without attracting any attention she needed to go through the side entrance instead of the main lobby, but it had a key card entry and she wasn't a guest.

It was eight o'clock in the morning, a veritable rush hour for hotel guests loading up their cars and checking out. Sena knew from experience it wouldn't be long before someone exited the hotel through the side door.

She was right. The door opened and out came a weary-looking mother carrying a wailing baby and dragging a toddler by the hand. She was followed by a pair of children already bickering about who got to sit by the window. Their father, weighed down by multiple bags over each shoulder, tugged a large suitcase behind him. At the car the parents argued over which route they would take, while the toddler whined about snacks.

Sena paused in the open doorway and looked at the family. She imagined how it would be to spend the day in the car with a group like that. Probably loud and uncomfortable. And wonderful. She felt a surge of envy. Then her stomach gave a growl and she turned to go into the hotel.

As she walked the long hallway to the breakfast lounge, Sena slipped some earbuds into her ears. She didn't have a music player to plug them into, but she'd noticed people were less likely to try to start up a conversation with her while she was wearing them.

Unfortunately, the earbuds didn't stop the guard from noticing her and kicking her out of the hotel that day. Sena wasn't sure what had given her away. She must have been careless…

She had hurried out the main entrance and put as much distance as she could between her and the hotel district, her stomach complaining at her the entire way.

Sena had heard the sirens before she saw them. When she turned the corner onto her block there were cop cars everywhere and people in hazmat suits going in and out of her front door, carrying out chemicals and equipment. Where was her mom? She scanned the crowd and finally spotted her, cuffed and sitting in the back of a cop car.

Great. Once they ID'd her mom they'd start looking for her too. Sena pulled up the hood of her sweatshirt and sat on the steps of the apartment building across the street. She knew she should get out of the area, but she thought it might be the last time she'd see her mom.

She watched her through the window of the police car, a tight feeling in her chest and a hot burning in her eyes. Who would hold cool cloths to her mom's head when she had one of her migraines? Who would make sure she ate?

Eventually, the scene quieted down and the street cleared out. The police car with her mom inside drove away. The yellow tape on her front door was the only indication that Sena's life was never going to be the same again. She stood and squared her small shoulders to face down the world.

Sena would survive.

Loud voices dragged her up from the depths of memories and sleep, leaving her feeling confused and dull. Ted and Kade were shouting. Ted held something in his hand and was shaking it in Kade's face. Kade looked ready to hit Ted. Danny and Claire were trying to calm the two down, and Sena attempted to understand what was going on.

As her vision cleared and she realized what was in Ted's hand, despair crept in and clutched at her heart.

Ted was holding the last of their water containers. All empty.

CHAPTER FOURTEEN

"WHAT IS WRONG WITH you, you stupid kid!" roared Ted. "You drank all the water we had!"

"You don't have any proof, it could have been anyone. Why are you picking on me?" Kade's voice was petulant, almost a whine.

"Do you think we're all idiots?" Ted's entire body shook with fury. "Look around. No one else could have done it without waking up the others."

"Two could have planned it together. They have the perfect alibi and I get blamed. It's not fair."

"What's not fair is that you've stolen *days* of our lives, all of ours. Days we might have reached land or been rescued. You're a murderer now, you know that? You might as well have stuck a knife in us while we slept." A dark gleam entered Ted's eyes. "Do you know what happens to murderers? From where I'm sitting, we're surrounded by an ocean full of death penalty. You're out of here."

Claire scrambled to free herself from the thermal suit. "Ted, wait. He's a kid."

"No, he's a *murderer*, and that entitled little brat isn't going to sit there and let us all die. He's going over the side." Ted got to his knees crawled toward Kade.

Kade's feet churned the space inside his thermal suit, trying to get a foothold and back away from Ted and the

124

entrance, but there was no escape within the limited confines of their rubber prison.

Claire was screaming and crying and clutching her husband's arm. He threw her off with such strength that doubt blossomed in Sena's mind.

"How do we know *you* didn't do it?" she asked.

Her softly spoken question penetrated the insanity in the raft and Ted glared at her angrily. "I wouldn't do that. I don't kill people."

"How do we know?"

Kade jumped on his last chance. "That's right, you didn't have anyone suited up with you either. The water is right next to you, so it would be easy. Way easier for you than for me, and since you're the leader you knew you could get everyone to blame the stupid jock. Real nice."

Ted looked at the others in disbelief. "You're going to take his word over mine?"

"There's no way to prove anything," Danny said diplomatically. "You might as well sit back down, we're not throwing anyone overboard."

The wind went out of Ted's sails, and he sat down weakly. He put his face in his hands and began to cry.

Claire attempted to comfort him while everyone tried to find something else to look at. Sena caught Kade's eye and he glanced away quickly, mumbling to himself about fairness and accusations until Lydia told him to shut up.

There was no food or water ration that day.

The next few days were windy and they prayed for rain, but the clear sky mocked their need. The entrance fly on the dome canopy snapped in the wind, making a tearing sound as the wind ripped it away from the velcro every few minutes and then blew it shut again.

Each time it opened, Sena stared out at the blue expanse surrounding them. It looked so good to her. She imagined scooping up the cool liquid in her cupped hands and bringing it to her face, water dripping from her chin as she drank and drank.

Danny told them all on the first day that if they drank seawater, the water in their bodies would be drawn away from their organs and blood to try to dilute the salty liquid. In short, it would kill them.

What if she didn't have any water left in her blood? Sena felt dry as dust. Surely, salt water was better than no water if she was on the verge of death anyway.

Claire noticed her gaze and put an arm around Sena. "I had a dream last night. My little boy was here with us and he said we shouldn't give up hope." Her voice was weak and papery. "Do you believe in a higher power?"

Sena shrugged, too weak to talk.

"This past year I've spent all of my energy hating God. I didn't know why he took my son. I thought it should have been me." Claire's cheeks were dry, but her voice was full of tears.

"I was so busy hating, I forgot about my daughter and husband. God only took one of my kids, but I've lost them both." Claire went on in her raspy voice. "I can't let it end this way. I have to live so I can tell Dee I'm sorry and show her how much she means to me."

Sena thought about her own mom. Was she out there somewhere, wishing she could make things right with her daughter? Did she wonder where Sena was and regret the years of neglect and abuse? Would her mom face down death for her, like Claire was doing for Dee?

Lydia reached over and squeezed Claire's arm.

"You're a good mum, and I know you'll make it back to your girl. Do you want to pray together?"

Claire nodded, and the two women clasped hands and took turns speaking their prayers aloud. When they finished, Lydia asked if anyone else wanted to pray. Sena shook her head. Kade and Ted declined too, but Danny said a few words. He prayed for strength to survive another day, and grace to accept whatever happened to them.

Sena prayed silently, forming a single word over and over again in her mind.

Water.

That night, Sena was awakened by something bumping into the raft. *Shark!*

Danny said sharks bumped their prey to see if it would fight back. If it didn't, the shark would attack.

They couldn't fight back. No one was strong enough to hit the shark with the oar. Even Kade had gone back to staring at the canopy. Heart racing, Sena waited for the shark to stop bumping and tear the raft apart.

Nothing happened. The gentle bumping was repeated every few minutes, but it looked like there would be no biting or screaming. She was awake now with no hope of falling back asleep. Her throat was filled with cotton and she could think of nothing but her thirst.

Sena dipped her fingers in the water that pooled on the floor of the raft wherever the weight of a body depressed the floor and then brought the moisture to her mouth.

Just a taste, she told herself.

The seawater was so good and wet. The saltiness didn't bother her at all.

She had to have more.

She tried to scoop water in her cupped hand but it dribbled out when she bent her arm. Her frustration filled her with anguish and she leaned her mouth to the water, intending to lap it up like an animal.

Claire stirred at her movement and caught her breath when she heard the sound of Sena's slurping. She pulled her back from the water, into the warm, bony contours of her body. "No baby, no, you can't…"

Sena fought like a wild thing, her ruined voice an unintelligible shriek. She would die without a drink. Did Claire want her dead? She clawed and kicked at the woman, feeling her matchstick legs behind her heels. Why wouldn't she let her go?

Claire held firm, and the fight drained out of Sena within moments. She didn't have the strength to move. Her whimpers filled the raft with the weight of her sorrow, but she wasn't ashamed.

When Sena opened her eyes again, daylight filtered in through the orange canopy. Nauseous, she leaned weakly against the side tube of the raft. She felt a soft bump.

"Did you guys feel that?" she rasped.

Weary eyes flickered in her direction then wandered away.

The door flap blew open in a gust of wind and she saw something floating in the water nearby. It bumped into the raft and the flap blew shut. She tried to process what she'd seen.

Office chair, said her deprived brain.

Danny had been right. She was hallucinating from drinking the seawater.

The bumping continued and she covered her ears,

though there was no sound. What was it, and why wouldn't it stop? It was driving her crazy. How could the rest of them stand it?

A horrible thought came to her. Maybe it was Charity's body, haunting them because they hadn't saved her.

Sena had to know what it really was.

The struggle to free herself from the thermal suit she shared with Claire was almost too much for her. Claire groaned for her to stay still and sleep, but made no effort to stop her. Bit by bit, Sena fought clear of the suit until she was free.

The cold water on the bottom of the raft was a shock, as was the wind that tore into her when she opened the flap and looked out.

She stared.

They were adrift in a sea of office chairs.

Sena blinked her eyes to clear them and looked again. The office chairs were still there, and so were a lot of other things. She saw broken pieces of wood, bags of charcoal, tennis balls, bowling pins, and a case of chapstick. The chapstick would feel so nice on her lips, she wished it wasn't a hallucination.

Then she gasped. A box of soy milk bobbed on the water, climbing up and flowing down the slow rolling surface of the sea.

"Kade," she whispered. He rolled away to face the back of the raft.

"Danny," she said. He opened his eyes and looked at her. "Do you see anything weird outside?"

He sat up, disturbing Lydia, who also sat up. His eyes widened. "Are those…" he paused to clear his throat, "…office chairs?"

Sena's body trembled. If the chairs were real, then the soy milk might be real too. She looked for anything she could use to bring it close enough to grab. The oar maybe?

It was heavy in her hand, and her weakened arm muscles strained with the weight of it. She forced herself to hold it steady and reached through the door of the raft, trying to stir the water and bring the box of precious liquid closer.

Her lips moved in a silent prayer. *Please.*

It was a slow, tedious process, the box inching toward her until a rogue wave lifted it and brought it bumping directly into the entrance of the raft. She leaned down and grabbed it, pulling it inside and cradling it against her chest.

It was real.

The soy milk was watery and cool in her mouth. It tasted like the leftover milk in the bottom of a bowl of granola cereal, and it coated her throat with a rich nuttiness as it went down. Even though she wanted to keep drinking, she stopped and passed the box to Claire after a few swallows.

Claire gave it to Ted, and Sena watched to see if he would pass it to Kade.

He did. They all studied Kade carefully, and after a few sips he passed it to Danny. The box of life-giving liquid made two complete rounds before it was gone. They looked longingly at the empty box in Lydia's hands.

When Ted asked, "Are there any more out there?" Sena couldn't believe she hadn't already thought of it.

She pulled at the fasteners that held the canopy to the raft until they came away and she tied the cover in its partially open position so they could all see out. The occupants of the raft gaped.

They floated in a sea of rubbish and debris... and salvation.

Drifts of apples, oranges and shoe insoles rose and fell with the motion of the sea. She saw bags of grass seed floating next to bags of whole walnuts. There were plastic bottles of every kind of oil she could think of, including olive oil, motor oil and baby oil. A couple of bags of flour nudged against boxes of wine and a case of Pepto Bismol, while bags of potato chips and cans of diet soda jockeyed for position on the waves.

There were also couches, end tables and wooden picture frames riding the swells, along with pairs of jeans, sweaters and an army of white crew socks and underwear. It was like Walmart had exploded in the middle of the ocean.

"It's a miracle," breathed Lydia.

"Let's get it," said Kade, with more spirit than Sena had seen from him in days.

In short order, they had a pile of food in the bottom of the raft, and they tore into it with groans of pleasure.

Sena bit into a ripe plum and its succulence exploded in her mouth. The juice dribbled from her lips and down her arms, while she devoured the sweet, moist flesh. She had never tasted anything so good.

Claire ate cherries so quickly Sena thought she had to be swallowing the pits, and Danny scooped guacamole dip from a container with an actual chip.

More quickly than she'd have believed possible, they were all replete with food. They leaned back against the tube walls, exhausted from their frenzy.

Where had it all come from?

Several theories were presented, and immediately dismissed as too far-fetched. Then Sena had a sudden memory of Mr. Stoddard's lecture onboard the *Duchess* about container ships. Excitedly, she told them what she remembered, about how they carried food, furniture, and much more.

"That might be true," conceded Ted, "but it doesn't explain how it all got into the sea."

"It could have been a boat crash," said Danny.

"Don't you think the containers would have just fallen overboard and sunk? What broke them open?"

Sena crawled to the opening to take some photos. Their good fortune was too incredible to believe. She wanted proof.

She saw lots of cans of soda and decided to focus on those for now, though she wondered why there was only diet soda. She saw two or three buckets floating nearby and realized they would be perfect for storing their food and catching water if it ever rained again. A large piece of plastic with a cheerfully bright yellow symbol on it caught her eye too. The black and yellow would make a nice contrast for a photo. She aimed the camera and waited for the waves to give her a better angle.

Alarm bells went off in her head when a wave tilted the plastic toward her and she read the word printed below the yellow symbol: *Radioactive.*

She clicked her picture and then realization dawned. She turned to the others. "I don't think we should eat any more, guys," she said slowly.

"Are you crazy?" said Kade, drinking a diet Coke. "This stuff totally saved our lives."

"Why not?" asked Claire.

Sena pointed at the sign on the plastic. Claire rose to

her knees to get a better look, and then she screamed.

It's not that *bad*, thought Sena. She looked back toward the sea and saw what had made Claire scream.

Floating in the cold water was the dead body of a man.

CHAPTER FIFTEEN

"WHAT SHOULD WE DO?" asked Claire.

"Nothing," shrugged Ted. "We can't do anything for him now."

"What about the food?" asked Kade. "Do you think it's radioactive?"

"I doubt it," Ted said. "I'm sure they don't really put radioactive materials on container ships."

Ted's words didn't make Sena feel any better. She remembered how Mr. Stoddard had said that container ship freight wasn't always checked or documented properly.

"You should get a picture of him," Kade told Sena.

"What? The body?" said Lydia, dismayed. "You don't need a picture of that. Give the poor chap his privacy."

Sena looked at the man, floating face up in the debris. His straight black hair floated away from his head in a halo. He was wearing a nondescript, dark uniform but his features were too swollen to make out. He might have been someone's dad or brother. Someone that would never know what happened to him.

Reluctantly, she snapped a photo of the dead man. Maybe someday it would help bring closure to someone. She turned away and realized Kade was staring at the body.

"Did you get a picture of him?" he asked.

Sena nodded. "How come?"

"Don't you recognize the outfit? That's the same thing the Koreans were wearing when they boarded the *Duchess*."

Sena spun around to get another look, but the body was already drifting away. "Are you sure?"

Kade shrugged. "I guess so."

"What does it mean?"

"I don't know for sure. I'd say they weren't ever on the airplane. I always wondered how they survived that crash. This makes more sense. They were from the container ship, and lied to the captain about the plane when he picked them up."

"Or he lied about where he got them."

"Could be," agreed Kade.

They both fell silent, thinking it over. If they hadn't been in the plane crash, then how had they gotten their burns? And why had the container ship sunk? Maybe they were sea terrorists, like pirates, blowing up ships and escaping. Sena knew her theory was a stretch, but couldn't come up with anything better.

She also realized with a start that she had photos of two of the men on her camera. If they ever got back to land she'd give it to the police. Maybe they could solve the case.

A sound from Danny made her look up.

"What I wouldn't give for a doody bag right now," he moaned, clutching his stomach.

All of them had eaten too much food, too quickly. Their deprived bodies couldn't handle it. Sena felt a gurgling in her own gut and was mortified about what was coming next.

The look Claire gave her was somewhere between

compassion and amusement. She gave Sena's hand a squeeze. "Don't worry, it can't be worse than dealing with the aftermath of bad chicken salad and I managed that once. I'll be right here with you."

The next few hours were some of the most agonizing, and possibly the most embarrassing of Sena's life. Of one thing she was certain—she'd never look Kade or Danny in the eye again.

As the occupants of the life raft recovered from the side effects of introducing food back into their diet, Sena slowly became aware that the days were getting warmer and the nights weren't as cold.

When she mentioned it, Ted nodded. "I think we're going to see land soon. Don't get your hopes up though."

"What's that supposed to mean?" asked Kade.

He and Ted had never repaired the rift between them, and Sena wasn't sure they would. Ted thought Kade was a spoiled, entitled teenager, and hadn't ever forgiven him for drinking their water. Even though Sena couldn't really blame Ted for having such a low opinion of him, she wished they would at least *try* to get along.

"If you must know," said Ted, "just because we can see it, doesn't mean we can get there. We're still at the mercy of the currents. Plus, depending on where we come in, we could be in for a rough landing."

Ted didn't say more. He didn't have to. Sena pictured their life raft being pounded into the surf at the foot of a rocky cliff, and from the looks on the others' faces, they were thinking it too. After everything they'd been through, they could still lose it all, and within a few yards of their goal.

When they finally did see land, it was just like Ted had predicted. They were at the mercy of the currents, and the currents didn't seem to want them ashore. They floated along within sight of land, but the green smudge in the distance didn't get any closer.

One night, Lydia asked if anyone knew what day it was.

"Monday, maybe? Or Tuesday?" said Danny. "Hey, I've got a one in seven chance of being right."

"No, I mean the date."

"Well, my odds are considerably worse on that. Maybe we can narrow it down."

They argued back and forth about the order of events until they finally decided they'd been on the raft for a little over five weeks.

Five weeks. Saying it made it sound so insignificant. Five weeks wasn't anything. It was shorter than summer break, or a typical science unit.

Five weeks on a life raft was *forever.*

"If we've really been on the raft for five weeks, guess what we missed," Danny said.

"Um, everything?" said Kade.

Danny shook his head. "The Fourth of July!"

"Big whoop," said Kade. "God bless the frickin' U. S. of ain't nobody bothering to rescue us."

"Whoa, you're not bitter or anything."

Kade shrugged. "Just saying what's true."

"You *were* listening when Mr. Stoddard told us about EMP's, right?" asked Sena.

"So there's a power outage, so what?" said Kade.

"We should probably talk about that," said Claire, with a glance at her husband. "Ted and I have been talking, and when we get back on land we don't think things are going to be the same as when we left. We could be facing total chaos."

"Oh please," scoffed Kade. "You're trying to scare us. It's not like there will be public lynchings or rioting."

Claire said, "No heroics, okay? I want everyone to be smart and stick together after we land."

If we land, thought Sena.

The landing, when it happened, was anticlimactic. They floated between green rocky shores for almost two weeks before a large landmass loomed in front of them. Danny thought they might be near the San Juan Islands north of Seattle.

The water pushed them toward a wide, narrow beach on their right, so Ted used the paddle to close the distance. When the water was shallow enough, they all struggled to get out of the raft and pull it ashore, leaning on each other more often than not.

Sena walked a few steps and then fell to her knees on the pebbly beach.

Danny laughed at her. "You're such a cliché, you know that?"

"I don't want to kiss it, I just can't make it stand still," Sena said. The ground seemed to move and roll beneath her.

"Don't worry, it'll wear off," he assured her.

She noticed he couldn't walk in a straight line either. "You better hope you don't have to pass a sobriety check."

The empty beach was surrounded by evergreens with a steep hill rising to tower over them. They were thankful it looked private and safe because they were too weak to explore. After more than a month of poor nutrition and inactivity, they could barely stand, let alone walk. They would have to spend the night there.

The beach was thick with driftwood and dry beach grasses, and Kade and Danny gathered fuel. Though the day was warm, they all agreed a fire would be nice.

Danny was the only one in the group that had ever done much camping, and he showed all of them how to roll the dry grasses between his hands until they formed a loose clump of a bundle. He set that down on a flat piece of driftwood and made a pile of twigs and small sticks close at hand. He said the trick at first was not to overwhelm the tiny fire.

Ted handed him the matches from the emergency kit and Danny struck one. Nothing happened. He tried again and the match head crumbled. The matches were ruined.

There was a collective sigh of disappointment. "A fire would have been so nice," said Lydia.

"Don't give up the ship," said Danny, and then cringed. "Sorry, bad choice of words. I just mean there's more than one way to skin a cat."

"Danny!"

Kade smirked. "If we had a fire and a cat, I'd skin it."

"Then the cats had better watch out, because I'm going to get this fire started tonight," Danny said determinedly. "Didn't I see you with some reading glasses, Ted?" He squinted at the sun. "It's a clear day, and we can use the lenses like a magnifying glass."

"You can use mine," said Sena.

"I don't think so," said Danny. "Aren't you near-sighted?" Sena nodded. "Sorry, they won't work. When light goes through your type of lenses it disperses or spreads out. Reading glasses focus the light and bring it in to a small point."

"How do you know that?" asked Sena.

139

"My dad and I used to do some camping together. He was far-sighted."

Danny gazed at the bundle of grassy tinder for a few moments longer than necessary, and Ted finally had to touch him on the arm to get his attention. Danny took the glasses and held them out so the sun shone through the lenses. Tiny pinpricks of light focused on the sand. "Yep, these will work." He moved the lenses until one bright spot was on the bundle of grass, adjusting the height until the circle of light was as small as he could get it. Within thirty seconds, Sena saw wisps of smoke rising from the tinder.

Danny leaned down and put his hands behind the grass and blew steadily into it. The smoke increased, until tiny fingers of flame appeared. Danny made a mouse-sized teepee of twigs around the fire, and when they were burning, he made an even bigger teepee, and then set bigger pieces of wood around the outside in a square, like a log cabin. "We'll push those in as it burns. That ought to last for a while."

Sena drew her knees up, rested her chin on them, and stared into the flames. It was good to rest on solid ground in front of the fire, listening to it snap and spark, and hearing the lapping waves behind her. She finally felt safe.

Claire sat nearby, and Sena moved closer to her. A feeling of total contentment washed over her. There was nowhere else she wanted to be, nothing else she wanted to be doing. She was totally content to be safely on dry ground with her friends.

They spent a couple of days and nights on the beach, getting their strength back and discussing plans. Kade was angry at the delay, but he didn't push. He was the strongest of all of them, and even he moved slowly.

Everyone was anxious to find out where they were and the state of things back home. It didn't appear things were good. Boats and jet skis should have filled the sparkling, smooth waters in front of their beach, but they hadn't seen a single person. Sena felt a pit of dread in her stomach when she thought about what that might mean, and even Danny's optimism waned.

Bit by bit, they became steadier on their feet until Ted announced they would leave the next day. Trying to decide what to bring was difficult because they didn't have a good way to carry anything.

Sena's backpack was filled with food, and although Kade offered to carry it, they decided it wasn't a good idea to give him all of their food. Kade pouted and went to scout out their trail.

Claire said they'd need the winter clothing they'd scavenged from the container ship for the journey to Lookout Falls. It was hard to take her seriously though, with the warm summer days and temperate nights. Who wanted to lug around a winter coat in August?

At the point it felt like they'd be delayed until winter since everyone had a different opinion, Lydia came to the rescue. She took the knife from Kade and cut several square pieces of orange nylon from the life raft. Inside, she placed a thick jacket and pair of gloves, and then wrapped up the bundle and tied it to a stick.

"Like a hobo!" said Claire. "Brilliant."

Soon everyone had their own hobo bags, and they were off.

In Kade's explorations, he'd found a trail leading to a parking lot and a road, so they started there, following the deserted road north. Their progress the first day was slow, and they didn't see any signs of civilization until evening.

They had just climbed to the top of a hill and Sena hoped Ted would call it a day and let them rest, when below them, they could see a large expanse of water and a bridge stretching from their side over to the other. Two run-down businesses huddled at the foot of the bridge, more like shacks than buildings.

Signs in front of the first offered fresh blackberry pie, fresh eggs, cold watermelon and homemade ice cream. The other business was a combination boat rental and antique store.

Sena's mouth watered at the thought of warm blackberry pie and homemade ice cream, but her hopes were dashed when she realized both businesses were closed.

Danny hurried ahead. "You never know until you try," he called back over his shoulder. He peered into the windows of the fruit stand and then shook his head at them. He wandered around behind the second store and a few minutes later he reappeared.

On a bicycle!

He rode around in the parking lot until they reached him, ringing the bell cheerfully. When they were closer he said, "There are more in back. It's a rental place."

Sure enough, there was a rack containing eleven bikes.

"I'm surprised they aren't locked up," said Claire.

"They were," said Ted, holding up a chain. "Someone was here before us and cut them loose."

Meanwhile, Sena made the best discovery: a water spigot protruded from a pipe outside of the store. They'd only had soy milk and diet soda for two weeks. She said a small prayer and pumped the pump handle up and down.

Clean water came gushing out of the spigot and she laughed. She let it spill over her hands and splashed it on her face. Soon they were all standing around the spigot, taking turns pumping for each other and letting the water fill their cupped hands and loudly slurping it up.

Ted had made them save their empty soda bottles for this exact thing, and now they rinsed and filled them with water. "We'll stay here tonight and get a good start tomorrow," he said.

Even though the sun was too low for Danny to make a fire with Ted's glasses, the night was warm and they used the clothes in their packs for bedding.

While everyone ate their ration of fruit, Danny announced, "I'm pretty sure I know where we are. We went right by this place on our way out of Seattle. I recognize the bridge."

Sena thought she could remember seeing the bridge now too.

"Didn't you guys say you go to school in Arlington?" Danny asked. "If I'm right about where we are, it's only about twenty miles from here. We should be able to get you home in a day or two."

CHAPTER SIXTEEN

HOME.

THE THOUGHT WAS enough to keep Sena tossing and turning through the long night.

After finding out they were so close to Arlington, Claire and Ted immediately started talking to Lydia about her travel plans. They wanted her to come with them to Lookout Falls where Claire's grandfather and daughter were living, but Lydia wanted to head south to her apartment in Seattle to see if her neighbor was still taking care of her dogs. She said she would have nightmares for the rest of her life if she abandoned them. They were like her babies.

Sena contemplated her own plans. She hadn't told anyone about her foster family's trip to California. For all anyone knew, they were at home waiting for her.

For a minute she fantasized about staying with Claire and Ted. She'd grown closer to Claire during their ordeal, and she liked Ted too. The couple suited each other and she liked how dedicated they were to their family. They were determined to get back to their daughter, despite the fact that they had no money, transportation, or supplies. Not once did they give way to doubt.

She thought about her own mom. Had she ever felt the same about Sena as Claire felt about her daughter?

Sena got out the most recent letter her mom had sent her. Although it had gotten wet, Sena had it memorized. In it, she told Sena she was approved for parole. She said she'd done everything she could to get out early for good behavior so they could spend Sena's senior year together. She'd already arranged a place for them to live, and she promised things would be different.

Sena believed her. She knew it was naive of her to take her word for it, but if her mom was really off drugs, she'd be different. She'd want a daughter to go shopping with and watch old movies together. She didn't have to be perfect, she just had to want Sena.

Was that too much to hope for?

Sena was afraid her restlessness would awaken Claire, however, the woman didn't stir. Her soft snores next to Sena in the darkness were familiar and comforting, but sleep was still a long time coming.

Much too early the next morning, Sena awakened to the sound of shouting. Squinting, she felt around until she found her glasses. She didn't need them to know Kade and Ted were at it again.

"You just have to be the big boss, don't you?" accused Kade.

"If that's what it takes to get some sense into your thick skull, then yes, I'll be the big boss."

Sena whispered to Lydia, "What's going on?"

"Kade wants to go ahead without us. He says he can make it home from here by himself and we're slowing him down."

"Ted should let him go," said Sena. "He's been a jerk ever since Charity died."

Lydia nodded her agreement. "I don't think he's going to have any choice." Sena could see she was right. Kade tied a few bottles of water to his bike frame, and then he was ready to go.

"Kade, let us ride you home," Claire pleaded. "We still don't have any idea what we're going to find when we get back to civilization."

"Speak for yourself. I'm going to find home-cooked meals and hot showers." He got on his bike and looked around at the group. "Good luck, guys. It's been real." He pushed off and pedaled toward the bridge, alone.

After he left, Danny told the group, "I'm going as far as Sena's house, and then I've been thinking I'll help Lydia get to Seattle. I don't have any family here, and I don't think she should go alone."

Ted looked up at the sky, and shook his head, an expression of disbelief on his face.

"It's safer if we stick together," said Claire. "I'm sure Lydia's dogs are fine. You should all come with us."

"I don't want to keep you from your daughter any longer than necessary," said Danny. "I'll be fine."

When she saw Claire looked prepared to fight, Lydia interrupted. "Let's work it out later. There are still miles to go, and I'd like to get started."

The way was slow and hard. No one had the endurance to ride far, so they walked their bikes up hills, and took frequent breaks in the shade.

Gradually, the area began to show signs of civilization. Abandoned cars littered the shoulders of the road, and as woods changed to farmland they occasionally saw people working in the fields.

Although Sena wasn't a farmer or gardener, she could see the crops weren't doing well. Shriveled, brown plants bent to the ground in unhealthy obeisance while farm machinery stood idle in the fields.

It took some convincing from Claire before Ted finally agreed they could stop at a farmhouse and try to get some information. "You guys stay back by the road," he instructed. "If there's any trouble, you get out of here fast, don't wait for me."

The farm they approached was bordered by a split post fence with rusty nails holding rustier barbed wire in uneven rows. A large barn sagged nearby, and on its weathered gray wood a hand lettered sign read, "Well rotted horse manure for sale." The word "manure" was crossed out.

Ted hollered to the house, "Is anyone home?"

A window next to the door opened slightly and they saw a woman with a rifle. "What do you want?"

"Just information. Can you tell us what the date is or where we are? Are you experiencing a power outage?"

The woman's laugh was a harsh bark. "Yes, we're experiencing a power *outage*." She spoke the word with a sneer. "We're also experiencing a food *outage*, a water *outage*, a government *outage*, and a humanity *outage*. And, if you don't get moving, you're going to experience a life *outage*."

From her position at the gate, Sena noticed movement in one of the upper windows. A figure stood almost lost in the shadows, nothing to give them away except for a slight flutter of the curtains as they were parted by the barrel of a gun.

Ted raised his hands, palms out, and took several steps back. "I understand, we don't want any trouble. Can you tell me what month it is, or what day?"

"Look around, Mister. It's the Day of Reckoning."

Back on their bikes again, the group rode until Claire

broke the silence. "We should probably start looking for a place to sleep tonight."

Sena noticed something coming toward them. "Hey guys, look. Is that a bike? Maybe it's Kade."

A closer look told her it wasn't Kade. From far away, the cyclist looked like a huge man, but as he approached, Sena realized he was an average-sized man carrying a huge load. From the front she could see the enormous backpack he wore. It was stuffed full, and he had camping gear lashed to the frame of the bike.

He rode past, not even glancing in their direction. From within the biker's windbreaker, wide blue eyes stared out at them, and Sena realized he had a small child strapped to his chest.

"Did you get a load of that guy?" asked Sena, turning to watch as he quickly lengthened the distance between them.

"Did you get a load of his bike?" asked Danny, also turning to look.

Sena hadn't yet glanced at the bike. Now she did, and realization hit her like a punch to the stomach. She glanced hurriedly back at Danny, her mouth hanging open in surprise.

Danny answered her unspoken question. "Yep, I'm pretty sure that was Kade's bike."

"Should we go after him?" she asked.

"And do what?" said Ted, tiredly mopping the sweat from his forehead. "If we could catch up with him, which is unlikely in our current condition, he's bigger and he's got a lot to lose. He's probably armed too. I couldn't win that fight."

"We don't have any way to get the bike back to Kade anyway," said Claire. "Let's stick to our original plan.

We'll make camp here, and look for Kade first thing tomorrow."

Sena hoped he was safe somewhere, but she didn't think he would have given up his bike without a fight.

Their supplies were running low, so they ate shriveled corn straight off the cob and then bedded down in the rows between dry, whispery cornstalks.

Sena's thoughts turned again to her mother. In a few days they would be reunited. Would she be happy to see Sena? Would they be able to build any kind of a life together in a world that was falling down around them?

A speck of light traced across the sky, grabbing her attention. Sena had never seen so many stars. There were so many, it seemed like a bright blanket had been thrown over her. In the total absence of electric light, the Milky Way spilled across the sky in a broad, twinkling expanse. The enormity of the universe made her problems seem small and insignificant.

When she closed her eyes to sleep, a million pinpricks of light continued to dance above her. They shone down on a once prosperous nation, now starved and desperate to survive. They shone down on darkened cities where they hadn't been seen for generations. And they shone down on a small farm in northern Washington where another teenage girl thought about her own mother and wondered where she was and if she'd ever see her again.

The next day they made slow but steady progress. By late afternoon as they approached the outskirts of Arlington, they finally saw Kade. He limped slowly along beside the road, and when they pulled up to him Sena's heart wrenched at the sight of his injuries.

His dingy t-shirt was torn, leaving a bruised shoulder exposed, and one of his eyes was swollen shut. She'd had a few black eyes of her own, but never one so enormously purple. His arms and face showed bruises and scratches, and he clearly favored his left leg.

"Oh, Kade," said Claire. "You poor thing. We never should have let you go off by yourself."

"I was outnumbered," he muttered.

Danny and Sena exchanged a quiet look. Even Ted kept his mouth shut.

"We're stopping here," Claire announced. "Let's get you cleaned up," she said to Kade.

It was still early enough to make a fire, so they made camp and then roasted their last three apples on sticks over the coals. Sena and Kade sat a little apart from the others and shared one of the apples. After passing it back and forth a few times Sena said, "You can have the rest, I'm full."

"You only had three bites, there's no way you're full."

"Yes I am. I think my stomach shrunk. I couldn't eat another bite."

"What if it was hot apple pie with ice cream?"

Sena's mouth watered and she swallowed loudly.

Kade laughed. "See? Have some more and pretend it's apple pie."

"No, you should finish it. I'm going to be home by this time tomorrow."

"Well, so am I," said Kade. "Come on."

Sena shook her head.

Kade's eyebrows lowered and he glared at her with his one good eye. "Why do you have to be so nice all the time? You make me feel like a jerk."

Sena was surprised by his sudden anger. "What are you talking about? You're not a jerk. You've just had a hard time lately."

"Don't lie. Everyone here hates me." Kade glanced at Ted and lowered his voice. "You know it was me. I drank the water."

"Oh, Kade, you can't keep blaming yourself for that. We were all out of our minds with thirst. I probably would have done it if you hadn't."

"No you wouldn't. I've seen what you're like. You help people, even when they take advantage of you."

"You help people too! What about when you went into the fire with me to look for my roommates? And when you brought me the batteries? Why are you being so hard on yourself?"

"I'm just being honest. You live in a bubble where everyone is nice and helpful. Well, the world has changed. Wake up and smell the apocalypse, Sena. It's time you see that it's everyone for themselves now."

"I offer you a few extra bites of apple and now you're freaking out on me? It's just an apple, *Kade.*" She emphasized his name, anger beginning to glow in her chest.

"It's not *just* an apple. It's the last of your food. Where are you going to get more? Do you think you're going to find another container ship to save you? Can't you see what things are like now? You should spend more time looking out for yourself."

"Like you did? How did that work out for you?"

"Am I supposed to let a bunch of strangers slow me down?"

"Strangers? Is that what you really think? After everything we've been through?"

"Stop trying to act like we're friends. I didn't know anyone else on that raft except Charity." Kade's voice cracked when he said Charity's name. He turned away and rubbed at his good eye.

His tears touched something in Sena and suddenly she didn't want to fight any more. "I wish she was here. She'd make you see sense. You *are* a good guy, Kade. You could have gone on the lifeboat but you came back to help her."

"Charity was…" he trailed off and Sena didn't think he would say anything else, but then his words came out in a rush. "I loved her, Sena, and I didn't tell her. I didn't know it for sure until after she was gone. I've hated myself every day since then. All the times I flirted with someone else to make her jealous, or I pretended I wasn't interested so she wouldn't guess how much I liked her. It was all stupid. I'm stupid. A stupid jerk. And it should have been me that got shot instead of her."

Sena searched for something to say, but Kade's words had stunned her.

Finally, she said, "Are you saying that back on the ship, in the ice cream freezer… that was for Charity's benefit?"

Kade sighed. "I told you I was a jerk. I'm sorry, Sena. After tomorrow you can forget you ever knew me. You deserve real friends."

He retreated to the opposite side of the fire and curled up on his side in a pile of dried pine needles beneath a tree. When Sena looked back to where he'd been sitting, she saw he'd left the apple for her.

CHAPTER SEVENTEEN

SENA LOOKED FROM THE number on the house back down to the letter her mom had sent and then turned over her shoulder to the rest of her group. "All right, this is it. You guys can go. I'll be fine."

"First I want a hug," said Danny. He and Lydia were heading to Seattle after they dropped Sena off.

"I'm gonna miss you," Sena said into his shoulder. "You've been like a brother to me."

"I'll come check on you after we're done in Seattle," said Danny, releasing her.

Sena hugged Lydia too. "I hope your dogs are okay."

"I know I'm crazy," said Lydia. "They're like my kids though."

Sena moved to hug Claire, but she said, "Before we say goodbye, I'd kind of like to meet your foster family."

Sena hadn't told anyone she was taking them to her real mom's house.

Ted added in a firm tone, "We aren't leaving until we know everything's okay and you'll be safe."

Apart from a few visits to the prison, it had been over four years since Sena had seen her mom, and she wasn't thrilled at the idea of having an audience for their reunion. It didn't look like she had much of a choice though. Reluctantly, she raised her fist and knocked.

The door opened a crack and a bloodshot eye peered

out at her.

"Mom?"

"Sena?" said the woman, opening the door wider. "Sena!" She flew from the house and embraced Sena in a tight hug before stepping back to hold her at arm's length. "I can't believe it's really you."

The woman was small, thinner than her malnourished daughter. Her black hair hung in dull tangles around her face, which was marred by acne and scars. She smiled at Sena, revealing black and yellow nubs of teeth.

Sena took in her appearance and her heart sank into the depths of her soul. She wondered how much the others had seen and understood. She turned to tell them to go and saw shock and surprise on almost every face. Claire's eyes were filled with an emotion Sena couldn't read.

"Is this your real mom, then?" she asked gently. She stepped up onto the patio and introduced herself.

"I'm Songyee," said Sena's mother. "Thank you for bringing my daughter to me. When she didn't come home from the cruise I thought she must be dead."

"Who's out there, Song?" slurred a male voice from inside the house. "Tell 'em we ain't got nothin."

Sena's heart skipped a beat. "Who else is here, Mama?"

"I met him down at the pharmacy a few weeks ago, his name is Conley. I invited him to come by, and he's been here ever since."

Moments later a shirtless man pushed Songyee to one side and blinked in the bright afternoon light. He was taller than Ted, but the skin on his shrunken chest clung to his ribs, and his pants hung from bony hips. His head was shaved and he had a tattoo of an angry black skull on the side of his neck.

"What's goin' on out here?" he asked.

"It's my daughter," said Songyee. "She's come home to me."

"Is that the brat you're always crying about? Well good, maybe now you'll stop being such a buzz kill and we can have a little fun around here."

He looked hungrily at Sena and she forced herself not to wither under his oily gaze. She turned back to her mom. "You said it would be the two of us."

"I told you, I didn't think you were coming back. You have no idea how lonely I was. Conley's been helping me, and I help him. He needs me."

"But Mama, *I* need you."

Sena hated the neediness in her voice and the tears that threatened to spill down her cheeks.

"I'm right here, baby." Songyee reached a hand out to Sena. "Come on in and we'll all get to know each other."

Conley licked his lips. "That sounds like a real good idea."

Something touched Sena's hand. It was Claire. She pulled Sena to one side and told her in a low voice, "I can't leave you here like this. Come and live with us in Lookout Falls. Ted and I already love you like a daughter. Please come with me."

The warmth of Claire's arms around her strengthened Sena. She wanted to believe her, but after four years in the system she knew that foster families didn't work out. What if Dee didn't like her? Claire would choose her real daughter over Sena, and then Sena would be left to fend for herself.

She glanced over at Songyee, who was studying the pair carefully. Maybe she had changed after all. She'd called her "baby," and Conley had said she cried over Sena.

"I'm sorry," she told Claire. "Even though you've been great, I have to stay here with my mom."

Claire's face fell, and Sena knew she wanted to argue, but she didn't want a scene. She stood next to her mom and waved at her friends. "Good luck on your trip, guys. Thanks for getting me home."

Everyone looked unhappy and reluctant to leave her there. Even Kade, who she'd thought would be the first to head for his own house, stood his ground and glared at Conley.

"Maybe we could come in for a few minutes and Sena could show us her room," suggested Claire.

"You think I'm stupid?" Conley growled, brows drawn low and eyes hard with suspicion. "I work my butt off for what we have and I ain't gonna let no one take it."

Ted scowled. "Are you implying that my wife would try to rob you?"

"It looks like she wants to take the girl. You folks need to get on your way."

"Thanks for bringing my daughter to me," said Songyee. "Maybe you can come back another time."

No one moved until Conley reached behind his back and pulled a handgun from the waist of his jeans.

"I said you should leave. Now."

Claire looked pleadingly at Sena but Ted grabbed her hand and led her away. She turned to look over her shoulder for one last try. "Bring your mom, she can come with us. My dad has plenty of rooms in his house, you can be with your mom and we can help her."

"That's enough!" roared Conley. "She don't need your help." He waved the gun wildly and Sena's friends hurried to get on their bikes. Sena turned back to her mother and didn't watch as they rode away.

The first thing that hit Sena as she walked into the house was the smell of cat pee and chemicals. The second was Conley. He slapped her bottom when she walked through the door behind her mom.

"Your mom never told me you were so pretty or I would have helped her look for you."

"Leave her alone," said Songyee in a tired voice.

"You looked for me?" said Sena, moving away from Conley.

"I tried. I went to the school, but no one was there. Your foster family wasn't home, and I didn't know any of your friends."

"She was real sad when she couldn't find you," Conley said. "Real sad. Lucky for her she met me. I helped take her mind off her troubles."

Sena looked around the room and had a pretty good idea how her mom had been distracting herself from her troubles.

The small house had an open floor plan, so she could see into the kitchen from the living room. It was cluttered with glassware and aerosol cans, jugs of household cleaners, batteries, and buckets of murky liquid.

It was a meth lab, practically straight out of her childhood, with one notable difference: a full-sized gas barbecue grill.

"Why's that in the house?" she asked her mom. "That's dangerous."

Songyee shrugged. "Not any more dangerous than having a stove in the house."

"How else are we gonna cook our food without

157

electricity?" said Conley.

"Mama, it's way more dangerous. Do you want to burn this house down too?"

"Don't you use that tone with me. I'm doing the best I can, and I don't need you judging me."

Sena clamped her mouth shut. She wanted to help her mom, not fight with her. "Can I see my room?" She imagined the book lined room her mom had promised her.

Songyee shifted from one foot to the other. "I was thinking you could sleep in here."

Sena looked around the living room. Trash covered every surface. Plastic bags, stained cardboard boxes, and torn or crumpled paper lay scattered across the floor.

It appeared they'd just tossed empty jugs and jars out of the kitchen when they were through with them, not bothering to put the lids back on. Some were broken and others spilled foul contents on the carpet, leaving stains and shards of glass in the old shag.

Songyee went to a sagging couch in the corner and pushed a mountain of dirty clothes onto the floor. "Give this a try, it's real comfortable."

Sena noticed a musty, damp smell when she sat down, and moved quickly to perch on the edge of the cushions. Her mom looked at her hopefully, so Sena said, "Thanks, I'm sure this will work."

Conley and Songyee stared at her in silence until Sena said, "Do you have any plans today?"

"I'm heading out to pick up a few things and do some trading. You stay out of the kitchen while I'm gone, you got that?" Conley said. "I've got everything set up how I want it." Without saying anything else, he went out the front door and slammed it shut behind him.

"Where's he going?" asked Sena.

"Oh... out. I don't know where he goes exactly. He usually brings back stuff we can cook."

Sena was pretty sure Songyee wasn't talking about food.

The thought of food made her stomach rumble, even in this foul-smelling room. She hadn't had anything to eat since the apple the previous day, and she was thirsty too.

"I know I just got here," began Sena, feeling awkward. "But do you have anything I could eat?"

Songyee nodded. "What's mine is yours. I'm afraid you won't like it very much though."

"I'll take whatever you have. I'm not picky."

Songyee's laugh was a bark. "That's what you say now. You haven't seen what I've got." She dug under the pile of clothes until she uncovered a threadbare backpack, and pulled out several things that looked like cans of tuna. "It looks like we're down to Tender Turkey Feast, Chicken Frick 'a Zee, and my personal favorite: Puka Puka Luau."

Sena's mouth fell open when she got a better look at the cans her mother was holding. Was she kidding? Sena glanced at her face; no, she was serious.

Songyee continued as if there was nothing unusual about suggesting her daughter eat canned cat food. "The Puka Puka is the best by far. It's made from real chicken."

Sena thought about the heyday Danny would have if he ever found out she'd eaten something called Puka Puka. "I'd be fine with an apple or a carrot or something."

"You are a stupid girl. No one has fresh food, and if

159

they did, they wouldn't trade it for crank."

Sena felt the sting of her mother's insult. She'd forgotten that about her. In her surprise, it took Sena a moment to understand what she meant. When she did she was shocked. "You mean you trade drugs for food?"

"How else would we get food? Do you want us to starve?"

"Isn't there some other way? What if you get caught? You could end up back…" Sena trailed off.

"Back in prison? Not likely. People need something to make them forget about their problems. They need the drugs."

"What will happen when they run out of food?"

"They are already out." said Songyee, indicating the cat food. "Lucky for them, the drugs make them forget their hunger. Forget their pain."

Sena saw her mother's eyes glaze over as she thought about the drugs.

"We should leave, Mama. We could go right now."

Songyee snapped out of her daydream. "Without Conley?"

"Yeah, just you and me."

"No, we can't. Conley makes the crystal. He makes the trades. Without Conley we'd starve."

"No we wouldn't," said Sena, an idea forming. "We need to catch up with my friends. Claire said there's room for us on her father's farm."

"Claire is the woman that brought you? You want to go back to her?" asked Songyee, with a sideways glance.

Sena looked at her hands. "I want both of us to go, Mama. You wouldn't have to live like this anymore. They can help us."

"You think I want to live like this? You think I want

my daughter to see me like this? If you would rather be with her than me just say so," Songyee snapped harshly. "Look at what kind of mother I am. You'd be better off with her."

Sena shifted miserably. "That's not what I meant. I think our chances would be better if we went with them."

Songyee rose to her feet, anger in the stiff lines of her body. "This is the life I can offer you. I know I haven't always been the best mother, but this is all I have."

"You don't understand," said Sena. "I don't care about the rest of this. You're my mom. I want to be with you."

Songyee's anger drained out of her, leaving her hunched and small. She reached a hand to Sena. "You're a good girl. We will leave in the morning and find your friends."

"Why don't we go now?" asked Sena. "Pack a bag and we can be on the road in a few minutes."

"I have things I must take care of first," said Songyee, turning away to shuffle down the hallway to her room. She stopped and looked back. "We will go tomorrow. I'm glad you are here. I missed you."

"I missed you too, Mama."

That night, Sena awoke suddenly from a bad dream and tried to remember where she was. One whiff of the foul stench in the house reminded her. What had awakened her? The house was quiet and Conley hadn't returned from his scavenging. Sena wore the tiny nightlight from her life vest on a thong around her neck, and she put it in her mouth to activate it. The light glowed in the darkness of the house.

161

Sena curled on her side on the lumpy sofa and tried to go back to sleep, but something felt… wrong to her. Was someone there?

She listened carefully. There was no sound, not even the sound of her mother's soft snores. "Mama?" she called. There was no answer.

Sena got up and gingerly picked her way across the trash-filled room. She was glad she'd slept fully dressed, including keeping her shoes on. She wouldn't have wanted to cross this floor with bare feet.

"Mama," she whispered again, pushing the bedroom door open.

In the glow of the tiny light she saw a small bedroom, cluttered with clothing and garbage. She moved carefully to the bed.

Songyee was perfectly silent and didn't stir when Sena sat down next to her.

Fear clutched at Sena's chest and she held her breath to listen.

Nothing.

"Mama?" Sena's voice was a strangled whisper. "Mama, wake up. We're going today. We're going to get you help. Wake up, Mama. Please?"

Still nothing.

Sena touched her mother's cheek, marveling at the sharpness of her cheekbone. She touched the side of her cool neck and then laid her head on her mother's chest. The arms that had seldom held her daughter remained at her lifeless sides.

All was still, except for the tears that slipped silently from Sena's eyes and fell unheeded on her mother's breast.

CHAPTER EIGHTEEN

SENA WAS STARTLED AWAKE the next morning. "Where did she put it?" demanded Conley. He dug through Songyee's drawers, tossing articles of clothing over his shoulder, then he cleared the top of the bureau with a single sweep. Perfume bottles and porcelain boxes fell to the floor with a crash.

Sena blinked puffy, tear-stained eyes and wondered what Conley was looking for, and whether he realized Songyee was dead.

She didn't have to wonder for long.

"The cow used the last of my stash to do herself in," he complained. He flipped an envelope at her. "It's Sena, right?"

Sena's fingers shook as she pulled a note from the already torn envelope, and read:

My dear Sena,

Thank you for coming home to me. You are a beautiful girl and deserve a better life than I can give you. Go to your new family and be happy. I love you always.

Mama

Sena crumpled the paper with numb fingers. She didn't understand. She didn't want a beautiful life and a new family. She wanted her mom and the life together she'd promised her.

Conley was pulling at the sheets and blankets on the bed, mumbling and ranting about his lost stash. Sena couldn't bear to see her mother's body in such disarray, so she stood to leave.

"Just where do you think you're going?" Conley straightened and looked at her with cold eyes. "If you hadn't come back and gotten Song all riled up, she'd still be here. This is your fault."

Sena flinched at the accusation. He was right. Maybe Songyee didn't have a very good life, however, she'd been alive until Sena showed up.

"The way I see it," drawled Conley, "you owe me. You got my cook partner killed and now I need another. I've got some guys coming to sample my product and thanks to you I ain't got no product. I'm gonna make a batch right now and you're gonna help me. Got it?"

Sena nodded. Wasn't this what she always did? She did what she was told. On auto-pilot, she followed Conley to the kitchen where he started sorting and measuring.

Was this going to be her life now? She'd take her mother's place in Conley's life?

"No," said Sena in a small voice.

"Did you say something?"

"No!" said Sena, shouting it this time. "I won't stay here and I won't help you make this stuff and kill more people."

Conley's face turned red. Sena was shaking all over and she could feel defiant tears slipping down her face. She wondered if he'd hit her, then she realized he was too much of a coward.

"Go on then, get out of here!" he shouted at her.

"You're useless, just like your mama."

Sena walked to the front door and sat on the step, breathing the fresh air. She was slightly lightheaded from the fumes, and she could still smell the foul odors from inside, so she stood and teetered down the sidewalk leading away from the house.

A blast of super-heated air hit her in the back and knocked her down. The sound of an explosion filled her ears and for a brief moment she felt the terror of being trapped on the burning cruise ship. As it had on the ship, the massive noise turned to a ringing in her ears that blocked out all other sound.

Sena got to her knees and looked behind her at the house. The blast from the explosion had blown out the living room windows, and flames licked at the curtains. Thick, black smoke wafted into the air and her lungs burned with the foul, acrid odor.

She rubbed her stinging eyes and tried to see Conley, but no figure emerged from the house and she considered briefly if her relief at not seeing him made her a bad person.

She crept down the sidewalk and across the street, where her legs collapsed and she watched the little house burn.

Neighbors from the surrounding houses emerged and stood in small groups apart from each other, whispering about the fire and what they knew of the people that lived there. Though there were no fire engines or police cars, Sena knew she needed to leave before she attracted anyone's interest.

Where could she go? Although her plans to leave with her mother had been vague and unformed, she'd at least hoped they'd have a backpack and some camping gear.

Now she had absolutely nothing except the clothes on her back and the meager contents of her pockets.

She thought about going to Charity's house, and realized she wasn't sure where she lived. Kade acted like he hated her; even if he didn't, she didn't know where he lived either. There was really only one place she could go.

Sena stood up on shaky legs, brushed herself off, and set off to find her foster family's house.

The city was not at all the way she remembered it from before the EMP and it was hard to know where she was once she lost sight of the pillar of black smoke from the meth lab fire she was using as a landmark. The streets were filthy and full of trash. Garbage cans in front of houses were filled to overflowing. Windows of businesses were broken or boarded over, and many houses were vandalized as well. There were a lot of cars on the roads, most of them abandoned.

Being alone in the town made her nervous, and the people she saw on the street intimidated her. They traveled in small groups and kept to their own territories, like gangs. She was the only one traveling alone.

Footsteps behind her set her heart racing. She glanced back and saw several teenage boys. One had already caught sight of her and he pointed her out to the others. Someone made a comment she couldn't hear and they all laughed before giving chase.

She darted into an alley and then across several parking lots. The laughter of her pursuers rang loudly in her ears and she knew she couldn't let herself be caught. They had the advantage of knowing this part of town better than she did, and she was terrified they would split up and corner her.

Ahead of her was a train station, and she hurried towards the open tracks. There wasn't anywhere to hide, and she pushed herself to a sprint across the tracks and climbed the chain link fence beyond. She dropped down on the other side and was halfway across the parking lot of a strip mall before the boys reached the fence. Ducking between two vans, Sena watched to see what they'd do. The boys paused at the fence, hands on knees, trying to catch their breath. When they turned back and left, she almost cried in relief.

Sena had taken refuge next to a family van, and on a whim, she tried the handle to the door. It opened. She climbed in and sat in the middle row next to a carseat and tried to get her bearings. She recognized the train station and had a pretty good idea where she was. At least she'd been running in the right direction.

After she caught her breath, she looked around the van. It had already been stripped of anything useful, and she was about to move on when she had an idea. Lifting the padding of the carseat, she discovered a treasure trove of old cheerios and goldfish crackers. She devoured them. Then she got down and felt under the front passenger seat. Sure enough, there was a half-full bottle of water. It was hot and stale. She guzzled it down.

Climbing out of the van, Sena thought fondly of the many times she'd had to clean up after the mess her foster sisters left in the family SUV. She nearly laughed. Who knew she was learning a survival skill?

Leaving her hiding place was difficult, but she didn't want to be on the streets after dark. The areas she passed became more affluent and residential, and now and then she saw children playing outside which reassured her.

They looked thin and grubby to her, and more skittish than children should be.

When she finally made it to her old foster home, she casually walked past it several times, trying to determine if anyone was inside. As dusk began to fall, she approached the house and tried the front door. It was still locked, which was a good sign.

Sena found the spare key tucked among the twigs that formed a "Welcome" wreath on the front door and let herself in. She locked the door behind her and leaned on it. In the fading light, the house looked exactly like it had when she'd last seen it, on her way to the cruise, the final conversations she'd had with the family echoing around her.

Jodie had been busy folding laundry and packing her kids' suitcases for their trip to California. Sena knew if she looked she'd find tiny stacks of neatly folded clothes tucked away in the upstairs drawers.

"Go give Sena a hug," Jodie had told her youngest. Five-year-old Tessa hugged Sena around the thighs and promised, "I'll bring you back a thoovy-neer." She was missing one of her front teeth and had an adorable lisp.

"Thanks, honey," said Sena, hugging her back. "I'll bring you something too. Maybe something from the North Pole."

"Really?" asked Tessa, her eyes wide.

"You can't take a boat to the North Pole," said Jamie, with the practicality of a seven-year-old older sister.

"Oh right, I forgot," said Sena. "How about I bring you a baby penguin then?"

"Wrong!" said Jamie, jumping up and down. "They only live at the South Pole."

Sena hid a smile and reached into her pocket for some

change. "I'll make you a deal. I'll find you something good, if you'll bring me back one of those flat pennies with Mickey Mouse on it."

"It's a deal," said Jamie.

"I want one!" said Tessa. So Sena had to look through her change again to find a shiny penny for Tessa.

"I'm going to miss you guys," said Sena.

Although they said they'd miss her too, Sena was certain they'd be too busy with rides and Disney princesses to think of her. They'd given her one last hug, and then she'd gone out the front door to get on the shuttle to Seattle.

That was the last time she would ever see them, or their parents. And now her mother was gone, and so were Claire and Ted and her friends from the cruise ship.

Sena was more alone than she'd ever been in her life, and the knowledge was stifling. Exhaustion overtook her. She climbed the stairs to her room with feet that dragged, and curled up on her bed with a heavy heart and fell instantly sleep.

She slept late the next morning, not waking until the mid-morning sun was full on her face. She stretched and luxuriated in the forgotten comfort of a soft bed and clean sheets. Was it possible the house hadn't been broken into since the EMP? Her good night's sleep made her optimistic, and she decided to go down to the kitchen and see if she could find any supplies.

She walked slowly, knowing if the kitchen had been looted she was in serious trouble. She had no food or water, no idea where to get them if there wasn't any in the house, and nothing useful to trade. For a brief moment she had a flash of understanding why her mother had gotten involved with drugs again. Just as quickly as it came, it was over. She would rather starve than do drugs or sell them.

Family photos caught her eye as she descended the stairs and she thought about trips she'd taken with the Clarks, particularly one camping trip to the mountains when she'd caught her first fish. Ross had taught her to clean it and then they'd baked it in tinfoil in the coals.

She wished she'd told him how much that had meant to her. The Clarks hadn't ever really warmed up to her. Not fully. They did their best. She should have been more thankful. She had her own room, plenty to eat, she went to a good school, and most of the time they included her in their family plans.

Sena paused in front of a piano covered with family photos. She'd planned to take a picture of the kids, but instead reached for a photo that included everyone, even herself. The Clarks had been her family for a while, and she wanted to remember them.

She removed the photo from its frame and tucked it into her pocket. Then, knowing she'd stalled long enough, she took a deep breath and went into the kitchen. Apart from a layer of dust on everything, it was pristine. Her heart began to beat faster when she pulled open the door to the pantry. Boxes and cans of food neatly lined the shelves, and two cases of bottled water were stacked on the floor below.

Sena laughed out loud at the sight.

After wrestling with the plastic shrink wrap on the water, she drained an entire bottle and then, out of habit, put the empty plastic bottle in the recycling bin. It clattered to the bottom and she wondered if there would be recycling again in her lifetime.

The fridge lurked in the corner of the kitchen. Would opening it be a big mistake? She braced herself for a wave of putrefied air and pulled it open.

Luckily, it wasn't *too* bad. Jodie had gotten rid of most of the perishables before leaving for their trip, so there were mostly condiments and things like pickles and a block of fuzzy green cheese.

Sena took a box of crackers to the kitchen counter and munched thoughtfully, trying to decide what she should do next. Now that she had food and water, she could survive on her own for a while at the house. Maybe for a few months if she was careful. Rationing food was second nature to her after being on the life raft for so long.

Her main concern was self-defense. She was certain it was only a matter of time before the house was broken into, if not by residents of Arlington, then by the masses of people that were sure to leave Seattle and come looking for food in the suburbs. Ross had owned a gun, but he kept it locked up in a gun safe and she didn't have the first clue how to get it out or use it.

She could load up a backpack with supplies and gear and try to find Claire's hometown. It was called Lookout Falls, and she knew it was somewhere east of Arlington on the 20. How could she carry enough food to get her over the Cascade Mountains though? She was sure she'd be robbed before she got out of town.

It had all seemed a lot more doable when she was trying to convince her mom to make the trip. Now that she was faced with going alone, she didn't think she could do it.

Additionally, Sena wasn't sure Claire and Ted really wanted her around. Once they got home they would focus on getting back to normal life with their daughter and they wouldn't want another mouth to feed, let alone another difficult teen.

To be honest, she wasn't sure she wanted to be with them either. She couldn't help blaming them a little for her mom's death. Songyee had thought Sena would be better off with them. Would she still have killed herself if she didn't think Sena had somewhere else to go? If only Claire hadn't hugged her in front of Songyee, and begged her to come.

Sena's anger at Claire boiled up. How did she think it would make Songyee feel, to see someone trying to take away her own daughter right in front of her? And what did Claire have to offer her anyway? A bed in the barn? A second fiddle role to her own daughter? Claire had said they didn't get along. Would anyone welcome Sena when her presence would likely only make that relationship more complicated?

She decided her best option was to stay in the Clark home for the winter. She'd stash the food and water somewhere people wouldn't think to look for them, and then see if she could make the house more secure. If someone broke in she would hide until they left.

Sena sighed and thought about how much work it was going to be to move all the food and find hiding places for it. She decided she deserved one day to recuperate from her ordeal. There was a stack of library books on her desk upstairs and she longed to lose herself in a story and forget about her problems, if only for an afternoon.

Five minutes later, she was curled up on her bed with a book, a bag of chips and a can of warm soda. She'd also found a working flashlight for when it got dark.

She just wanted one normal day. Was that too much to

ask? She would get back to the business of survival tomorrow.

It wasn't until Sena awoke at dusk from a long nap that she realized she'd made a big mistake. A normal day in her post-EMP world meant a constant fight for survival while never relaxing her vigilance. She had tried to justify a fantasy world of naps and library books back into existence, but it was turning out to be a normal day for her after all.

She could hear someone in the house.

CHAPTER NINETEEN

FOOTSTEPS SOUNDED AT THE bottom of the stairs, and she knew they'd find her soon. She sat up, heart pounding, and eyes darting all around her room. Where could she hide? The closet was probably her best bet, but it was so obvious.

Why had she been so careless? Planning for a break-in should have been the first thing she did. Now she was going to lose all of her supplies, and maybe her life if she didn't hurry up and get her act together.

She gingerly stepped toward the closet, praying the floor wouldn't creak, when a voice right outside her door practically made her lose control of her bladder.

"Sena, are you up here?"

Kade?

Sena's legs turned to flan and she wasn't sure they'd hold her up any more. She sat down quickly on the bed, which squeaked loudly.

"Is that you, Sena?" asked Kade, opening the door and pointing a flashlight right in her face.

She blocked the bright beam and complained, "Put that down, it's not dark yet. You're wasting batteries."

The blinding light was gone and Kade had her in a tight bear hug. "She's up here!" he hollered, right next to her ear.

Before she knew it, she was being passed from one hug

to another. It was kind of nice, though she was sorry not to see Danny and Lydia. "Did they really go to Seattle?"

Ted nodded. "We tried to talk them out of it, but there was no changing Lydia's mind. Thank goodness you're safe. You don't know what kind of a scare you gave us."

"You think you were scared," said Sena. Her heart was still racing. "Try having someone break into your house."

"We thought you were dead," said Kade.

"What? How come?"

"Maybe it was because the last place we saw you was a smoldering pile of rubble when we stopped by this afternoon."

"Oh, right." For a few minutes Sena had forgotten about the fire and Conley. And her mother.

Sorrow washed over her again. The bed creaked as Claire sat next to her, and Sena looked across into her eyes.

"Did anyone make it out besides you?" Claire asked gently.

Sena shook her head and let her hair hide her face.

"Why did it blow up, anyway?" said Kade. "Some kind of bomb? Was it the Koreans again? I've been thinking about them and I don't think they were just terrorists. I think they were it. You know. The guys behind all this."

Ted said, "Not now. Save your conspiracy theories for when we're back on the road."

"Are we stopping here for the night?"

Sena was surprised to see Ted and Kade interacting normally. Even respectfully. She wondered what had happened at Kade's house and why he was here with Claire and Ted.

Ted looked at Claire, who nodded. "I think that would be a good idea. We can load up the bikes tomorrow, and be on our way. Do you have a bike here, Sena?"

Sena felt a familiar warmth in her cheeks as frustration at being taken for granted brought hot tears to her eyes. She almost gave one of her typical, self-effacing responses but then her anger bubbled to the surface.

"Why does everyone assume I'll do what you tell me to do? Did you ever think maybe I have my own plans and they don't include going with you or outfitting your expedition?"

Claire's voice was soothing. "No one is going to steal your food or make you come with us. Just think it over tonight and you can decide in the morning."

Sena was itching for a fight and didn't check the words that spilled freely from her lips. "Why do you want me? So in case things don't work out with your real daughter you can use me as a backup?" She got a wicked satisfaction from Claire's flinch. "Well, maybe I don't want another failure of a mother in my life, if that's all right with you."

"That's enough," said Ted, in a tight voice.

Claire gave him a slight shake of her head and stood up. "We'll see you in the morning. I hope you'll decide to come with us." She sounded worn out. "I'm not that great of a mom, you're right about that."

Everyone filed out and left Sena to punch her pillow and try to figure out why she always screwed everything up.

A little while later there was a knock on her door. It was Kade.

"Hey listen," he said, leaning awkwardly on the door

frame of her room, "I wanted to say I'm sorry I was such a jerk."

"Which time?" asked Sena.

"I know I deserve that," he said. "All of them, I guess."

"Why are you being so nice all of a sudden? In fact, why are you here? I thought you'd be with your family."

"They split," he said. "We stopped by my house and they were gone. No note or anything, they just packed up all the food and took off I guess."

"I'm sorry," said Sena.

Kade shrugged. "We weren't that close anyway. Ted's been more of a dad to me than my old man ever was. It took my family abandoning me before I could see it."

Sena could hear the hurt in Kade's voice.

"Ted agreed to let bygones be bygones and give me another chance. I guess we'll see how it goes. So far so good." He took a deep breath. "We stopped by Charity's house too, did you hear?"

Sena shook her head. "Were they home?"

"Yep. Hardest thing I ever had to do," Kade said. "I don't really want to talk about it, but I thought you'd want to know."

"Thanks for doing that."

"I told her I would, you know? It was the least I could do."

"Well, I'd better get to bed." There was a pause and then Kade said, "There was one more thing I wanted to tell you. I was lying when I said you were a like a stranger to me. It's actually the opposite. You're like family. I'll miss you if you don't come with us tomorrow."

And with that, he turned and went out of her room.

Sena laid back down on her bed. She had a lot to

think about.

The next morning she found Claire and Ted in the kitchen eating cold instant oatmeal and poring over a map. "I guess I'll come with you," she said.

She'd thought long and hard about her options the previous night, and after experiencing what it would be like to have someone break into her house she decided she didn't want to spend the winter alone. Though she didn't want to admit it, she felt a closeness with Ted, Claire and Kade that she didn't want to give up.

Despite that, she was still angry at Claire and resented her for her mom's death. Maybe it wasn't fair, but it was better than thinking it was all her own fault.

"How did you guys find me here anyway? I didn't think anyone had this address."

"It was in your mom's address book. We found it in the glove box of a car parked behind the house."

Claire was about to say something else, but Sena never found out what it was because at that moment an engine roared to life and Kade whooped and hollered from the garage.

The Clarks' six-year-old Toyota Highlander still worked! They quickly turned it off and discussed how it might change their plans. They had hundreds of extremely difficult miles ahead of them, and with a working car they might be able to make the journey in a day or two, saving themselves weeks or even months of travel.

The excitement was contagious and Sena found herself smiling as they loaded food, water and camping gear into the back of the vehicle. They tied the bikes to the roof of the car in a tangled heap in case they ran out of gas and couldn't get any more.

Sena ran upstairs with a plastic garbage bag and thought about what to take. She filled the bag with toiletries and first aid supplies, and then stopped in the doorway of her room.

Sunlight fell across the bed, reminding her of the many Sunday mornings she'd tried to sleep in but Tessa and Jamie had different plans. They had jumped on her, giggling, and insisted she'd come downstairs and cook pancakes for them.

Sena sighed, knowing she'd probably never be back in this house again. What would life be like in Lookout Falls? Would she ever fit into a family again?

She gathered a few changes of clothes and looked around one last time. She didn't have much, so there wasn't much to take. She saw a copy of her favorite book, *A Wrinkle in Time*, on her desk and grabbed that too. The worn copy belonged to her, not the library, and she couldn't leave it behind.

Before she left, she snapped a photo of her room. Even though she knew it was unlikely she'd be able to develop the film any time soon, somehow it made her feel better about leaving.

On her way downstairs, she stopped in Ross and Jodie's room and took a good pair of hiking boots out of Jodie's closet and a couple of flannel shirts and some thermal underwear.

In the garage, everyone was waiting while Ted looked around with a flashlight for the manual release for the garage door.

"It would be just our luck if we found a working car and then couldn't get it out of the garage," said Kade.

With a loud squeak, the door rolled up and light

streamed in.

"All right troops, let's hit the road," said Ted, and with high spirits, they headed for Highway 20.

CHAPTER TWENTY

THE DRIVE WAS A lot easier than any of them had been expecting. A couple of months had passed since the EMP, so previous travelers had done most of the hard work of clearing stalled and abandoned vehicles from the roadway. Although they had to detour off road sometimes for a semi or long-forgotten car accident, the Highlander managed it without difficulty.

They saw other travelers occasionally; most were in cars or trucks too, while a few rode bikes or walked.

As they neared the mountains, rain beat down on the windshield, and they no longer saw any foot traffic. If people lived in the towns they passed, they weren't outside. The small communities felt like ghost towns.

Dull gray clouds blocked the view of the mountains, and the rhythmic sound of the windshield wipers lulled Sena to sleep. She didn't awaken until a few hours later when they slowed to a stop next to several vehicles on the side of the road.

"Why are we stopping?" asked Sena.

"We're getting low on gas," said Ted.

Sena looked out the window at the desolate stretch of road. "In case you didn't notice, this isn't a gas station."

Ted teased her. "Well, I'll be darned, you're right. Good thing I've got a back-up plan."

"Are you going to try and siphon gas?" asked Kade.

"I've got to see this."

"Siphon gas?" Sena queried.

"He's going to try to take the gas out of these cars and put it in the Highlander," Claire explained.

"And he's gonna get a mouthful of it in the process," said Kade, rubbing his hands together in gleeful expectation.

"Wanna bet?" asked Ted.

"Heck yeah. I siphoned gas out of my mom's car once, I know how it works."

Sena raised her eyebrows at Kade. "You stole your mom's gas?"

"She cut off my allowance! What did she expect? I wasn't going to just stay home."

"So how do you do it?" asked Sena.

"You basically stick some plastic tubing into the full gas tank, stuff a rag around it to keep any air out, and then suck on the tube until the gas starts to flow out. If you're fast, you can time it right, but most people get a mouthful of gas, like I'm betting Ted here's gonna get."

He turned to Ted. "What should the stakes be?"

"I don't know," said Ted. "I don't want to take advantage of you. The gas isn't going to get anywhere near my mouth."

"Do you have a hand pump or something?" asked Kade, narrowing his eyes.

"Nope, just some tubing and my mouth."

"You're so gonna lose," said Kade. "How about we bet our next dessert? The loser has to give his dessert to the winner."

"You're on," said Ted. Everyone knew he had a sweet tooth.

Despite the rain, everyone piled out of the SUV to

judge the bet.

Ted opened the back of the SUV and pulled out an empty gas can and a long length of half-inch plastic tubing.

"Where did you get that?" asked Sena.

"Your foster dad had a string of LED lights threaded through it. I found it mounted underneath the cabinets above his workbench. I think he was using it as task lighting. I'm glad I saw it. It's perfect for this."

Ted got out a pocketknife and cut the tubing into a five foot length and a two foot length. Then he went over to a pickup truck pulling a trailer with two jet skis on the back. He started climbing up in the trailer and Sena asked, "Wouldn't the truck have a bigger gas tank?"

Ted nodded. "Absolutely, but cars these days have valves and fittings down inside the tank that can make it really hard to get the tubing down to the gas. Getting gas out of jet skis, on the other hand, is going to be a piece of cake."

While he talked, he unscrewed the gas cap of one of the jet skis and poked one end of the longer piece of tubing down inside.

"Here we go," said Kade.

Ted didn't put the other end in his mouth, he put it in the gas can. Then he took the shorter length of tubing and put it in the gas tank of the jet ski too, though not as deeply. He pulled a bandana out of his pocket and stuffed it in around both tubes. Kade watched with a puzzled expression.

"Get ready to say goodbye to your next dessert," said Ted with a cheerful grin. He leaned down and blew into the shorter tube. No gas flowed, so he blew again, a little harder. This time Sena saw the fluid enter the longer

183

tube and heard it cascade into the gas can.

"No fair!" said Kade.

Ted slapped him on the back. "You live, you learn. I used to siphon gas out of my mom's car too."

The process took a long time. They were more than half finished when they heard the sound of engines approaching.

Ted's knuckles whitened on the gas can as they got closer and he told everyone to get in the car.

Claire and Kade did what he said. Ted stayed with the siphon, so Sena did too. She had discovered there was a power in standing up for yourself. After a few tense moments, a motorcycle gang roared into view from around a bend in the road.

Upon seeing them, Sena realized there was a proper time and place to stand up for herself, and this might not be it. She hoped they would pass them and keep going.

They didn't.

The group pulled their bikes in around the vehicles on the roadway. It was too late for Sena to go to the car now.

A fully helmeted gang member swung a leg over a bike. The rider was short and well-muscled, and wearing layers of worn leather. Sena noticed a little girl seated on the back of the vacated motorcycle.

Sena stepped closer to Ted and he put a protective arm around her. She looked up at him and he gave her a squeeze.

"Don't worry," he said. Then he turned to face the leader of the gang.

He exhaled with relief when the leader removed her helmet. It was a woman.

"So you're not one percenters?" asked Ted.

The question made no sense to Sena, but the woman shook her head. "Does it look like we're flying colors? Never were, and never gonna be. We're just a group of people trying to survive. Some of us are riding home, others are out looking for family. You don't bother us, we won't bother you."

"Sounds good," said Ted. "Could any of you folks use some gas? There's quite a bit left here and we already took enough to get us home. If you need a siphon I can let you use my gear."

The woman squinted at Ted. "That's real friendly of you. You looking for some kind of handout?"

"Nope. Just helping out a fellow traveler."

"We can use the gas, for sure, but we'll get it ourselves."

They started talking about the best way to get the gas out of the pickup, as the other bikers got off their motorcycles and stretched. Most of them were soaked from head to toe, and Sena thought they must be cold.

The young girl riding on the back of the woman's bike climbed down and walked over to her mom. She looked about eight years old, with dark, curly hair and a grimy face. She stared at Sena until curiosity got the best of her and she walked over.

"Is that your ride?" the girl asked, pointing at the Highlander.

The serious way she asked the question made Sena want to laugh. "Yep, that's my ride," she replied.

"Not bad," said the child, pursing her lips and nodding wisely.

"What's your name?" asked Sena.

"I'm Sassy," said the girl.

"That's your name?"

"It's from a book. You wanna make something of it?"

"No, definitely not," said Sena. "Do you like to read, Sassy?"

"A lot. I don't have many books though."

Sena pulled her copy of *A Wrinkle in Time* out of her back pocket and handed it to Sassy. "Here's a book you can keep. It's my favorite."

Sassy tucked the book under her jacket to keep it dry. "Are you sure?"

"I'm sure," said Sena. She noticed Ted was waving her toward the SUV. "I hope you like it," she called, and then climbed into the car.

"How far is Lookout Falls from here?" asked Claire when they were back on the road. "Do you think we could make it tonight?"

"It'll be way after midnight," Ted answered. "If we don't run into any problems, I think it's a good bet."

Claire's smile was positively radiant, and at the sight of it, a deep scowl crept over Sena's own face. She crossed her arms tightly across her chest and stared out the window. Despite her mood, the magnificence of the scene wasn't lost on her. They were driving through the North Cascades, the wildest and most rugged mountains she could imagine. Their imposing solitude made her feel very small.

Sena saw a waterfall tumbling down the rocky slope and pouring into an emerald green lake. If it hadn't been raining so hard she would have asked Ted to stop the car so she could take a picture of it.

A quiet, persistent internal voice reminded her that Ted and Claire probably wouldn't want to stop for photos anyway, when they were merely hours away from their daughter.

The road steadily rose higher, making tight hairpin turns and twisting back on itself. By the time they'd gone an hour past the green lake Sena was nauseous and miserable. She cracked her window open a little and inhaled crisp mountain air. It was sharp with the smell of rain and fir trees and she left the window down, despite the spray that wet her cheek and hair.

Soon she felt a little better, and noticed the rain wasn't coming down as hard. Ted slowed the windshield wipers and turned on the headlights.

"I think we're over the pass," he said. "We should be able to make good time now."

Dusk came quickly as the sun began to sink behind the high peaks at their backs. Ted increased his speed, saying he wanted to be off the mountain range before night fell completely.

Claire pointed to a speck high above them. "Is that a bald eagle?"

"I hear there are a lot of them here in the winter," said Ted, leaning forward over the steering wheel and looking up through the windshield. "I think you're right, I can see his white head."

Suddenly Claire inhaled sharply, the sound taking up all the available air in the vehicle.

Sena looked at the road and gasped too. Just before a sharp curve, an enormous boulder had rolled down the side of the mountain and come to rest in their lane. It was as big as a washing machine, and Ted swerved to miss it, but his attention had been on the sky, and the few short seconds he'd lost made it impossible for him to recover control of the car.

It clipped the side of the boulder, and the front tires

lost their grip on the wet road. The car careened sideways and hit the guard rail with a shriek of metal on metal that drowned out their own shrieks.

For a moment, it seemed the guard rail would hold them, but the force on it was too much, and it gave way with a loud crack.

The SUV hung suspended in the air for a moment, then flipped and bounced down the rocky mountainside. Sena's world spun and went dark.

CHAPTER TWENTY-ONE

THE DARKNESS PRESSED ON her eyelids like a weight. When Sena finally gathered the courage to open her eyes, the pure black of the night took her breath away.

Her head throbbed with pain and she tried to remember where she was. The air smelled thick and gritty and it was as dark as a coffin… or the closet she'd been locked in so many times.

She trembled uncontrollably and her teeth chattered. A groan nearby almost made her scream, but when she inhaled, her lungs filled with dust and she coughed instead.

"Sena, you're awake!"

It was Claire. Sena suppressed a sob of relief.

"Don't cry, honey. It's going to be okay."

Sena focused on the sound of Claire's voice and tried to control her panic. Her heart pounded against her ribcage and she heard the sound of shallow panting and realized it was her.

Deep breaths, she told herself, trying to understand her new reality. She was sitting in the SUV, and full night had fallen. She groped to her left and felt Kade's leg. When she touched him he didn't move or make a sound.

She needed to hear a human voice. "Claire?" she squeaked.

"Stay calm, Sena. Do you still have your flashlight?"

Her flashlight! Sena scrambled in her pockets and pulled out the slim penlight. It didn't do much to illuminate the darkness in general, but the tiny light was enough to show her the extent of their problems.

A quick look at Kade didn't reveal any blood or obvious injuries. He stirred when she shone the light in his face and looked to be coming around. Sena let out a breath she didn't realize she'd been holding.

"Can you shine it on Ted?" asked Claire.

Ted was slumped over, leaning on the deployed airbag. Sena reached out with a shaking hand and checked for a pulse. The beat was strong under her fingers and she exclaimed, "He's alive! He's okay!"

In the passenger seat, Claire began to cry.

"No, it's okay, he's alive. We're all alive." Sena couldn't believe their luck, but Claire kept crying.

"What's the matter?" asked Sena. Claire didn't answer.

"Claire?" asked Sena. She leaned forward over the space between the front seats and shone her light on the woman.

"Oh, no," whispered Sena. "No, no, no."

Claire was covered in her own blood. A rip in her shirt revealed a gaping wound in her side from which blood oozed freely.

Sena stared at it in shock. No, not Claire.

She popped open the storage area between the seats and pulled out a wad of napkins. She pressed them into the wound and Claire gasped.

"I'm sorry, I'm so sorry," said Sena. "We have to put pressure on it." It was like with Charity all over again.

The SUV was quiet as she held the napkins tightly against the wound, and she saw Claire's eyelids flutter.

"Stay awake," Sena ordered. "Tell me something about Maddie."

"Dee," whispered Claire. "She likes to be called Dee."

"Dee then. Tell me something about her. Why do you call her that?"

"Because her brother couldn't say Maddie. He called her Dee. I was so afraid she'd be alone, but Ted's alive. He can take care of her."

"Who will take care of me?" demanded Sena, with only the faintest quiver in her voice.

"Oh, Sena. You and Dee are going to be such good friends and Ted will take care of you both. Tell her I love her and I'm so sorry for this last year. I love you too, you know."

Claire's eyes closed.

"No!" shouted Sena. "I can't lose you, too!"

She climbed over Claire's still form and reclined her seat, then she checked for vital signs. Her pulse felt strong. She was alive, for now, and she needed help. They all did.

"Kade, get up," Sena shook him, hard.

"Ow, what?" mumbled Kade.

She shook him again, and this time he opened his eyes.

"Look at me," she commanded, and he focused on her.

"We've been in a wreck. Ted's alive, and hasn't woken up yet, and Claire's hurt bad. I'm going for help."

Sena was grateful to see understanding dawn on Kade's face. "No, I'll go," he said. "You stay and help." He turned to open his door and gasped in pain at the movement.

"What's wrong?" asked Sena.

191

"It's my foot."

Sena shone the penlight on his left foot. The shoe was in ribbons and she could see his foot was lacerated and swollen. "You're not going anywhere on that. Stay here and help Ted and Claire. Keep pressure on the hole in her side. If blood soaks through the napkins put more on and keep pushing on it. I'm going up to the road to look for help. You have to keep Claire alive. Got it?"

Kade nodded.

"I mean it, Kade. Keep her alive. Promise me?"

"I'll try, Sena. I promise."

She waited to make sure Kade knew what to do, and then handed him the flashlight.

"No, you'll need it out there," he argued. "It's so dark."

She set it down on the seat. "You'll need it more. I'll be okay."

Sena tried to open her door, and found it was blocked by a tree. She had to climb over Claire and through the shattered window to get out.

Kade moved into the spot between the seats and pointed the light at her.

"Sena, your head." He sounded worried.

She put a hand to the right side of her head and touched her hair, sticky and matted with blood. She didn't have time to worry about that now. "I'll be back soon," she said, and started up the mountain.

The moon was full, and the night was peaceful and cold. Even in the middle of the ocean it had never been so still and quiet.

It was also very dark.

Sena stood frozen in the shadows like a scared rabbit

192

too afraid to run. She wanted to hurry back to the SUV and wait for someone to find them, but she knew everyone was counting on her. Besides, no one was coming to help them. It was up to her.

She took a cautious step forward and shuddered when something tickled her face. She brushed it away and it stuck to her fingers. A spider web! Sena panicked, windmilling her arms in every direction and brushing frantically at her clothes.

After she calmed down, she giggled and was glad for once that phones weren't working. If anyone had filmed her spider dance just then she'd be an internet sensation for sure.

Laughing at herself pushed the fear away a little, and she looked around to see where she was. As her eyes grew accustomed to the dark she noticed the trail of broken limbs, branches and trees that marked the SUV's descent. She headed for it and began to climb.

The light of the moon cast a soft glow on the forest, though it did little to help her find her footing in the underbrush. She tripped over tangled roots and walked into tree branches. Thorn bushes caught at her clothing and scratched her hands and face. Every step was an ordeal, and she fought for every foot of progress up the hill.

She stopped for a moment to catch her breath, and turned to look down at the SUV. Its white paint gleamed in the dark forest, easily visible in the dim light. They'd fallen so far. It was amazing they were still alive.

Or, she hoped they all were. At the thought, she hurried back to the arduous climb.

Although the going was difficult, it was doable and she didn't have any real trouble until she was just below the roadway.

The drop off next to the road was steep, too steep to scale. She tried moving sideways along the roadway, but the SUV's fall had literally cleared a path down. Away from the path, the undergrowth was impossibly dense. Retreating down the slope wasn't an option. She had to find a way up, and quickly.

Sena began to climb the nearly vertical embankment, feeling for hand and footholds. The ground was wet from the rain, and wouldn't support her weight. She lost her grip several times, sliding down in the mud until she was caked in it.

She wanted to scream in frustration. It wasn't that high, only ten or twelve feet, but it felt like she was climbing a wall of pudding.

Sena made herself begin again, this time going more slowly and making sure with every advance she was firmly entrenched before she tried to go higher. She looked for some kind of handhold, and realized the broken guard rail was hanging down the embankment.

Careful not to unbalance herself, she reached up and grasped the rail. At that moment one of her feet slipped and she clung to the railing to keep from sliding down again.

It was sharp and jagged where the SUV had roughened its edges. The metal bit into her hand and tears of pain sprang to her eyes, but she refused to let go. She dug her feet into the embankment again and gripped the railing with her other hand.

Inch by inch, she climbed the last few feet to the top of the cliff, crying openly now as the jagged metal tore open her soft hands. Letting go meant failure, and she refused to give in to the pain.

Sheer determination brought her to the top of the road, and she sat on the cool pavement for a moment, catching her breath and wiping her tears before standing to face the mountain.

A chill breeze blew on her sweaty skin and she shivered. Dark trees with sinister shadows lined both sides of her path, and she heard strange sounds in the night. For a brief moment she wavered in her resolve. Silvery moonlight was bright on the ribbon of road before her, so she focused her attention on that and hurried down one of the highest passes in the Northern Cascades.

Sena was soon winded and had to settle for a slower pace, managing a brisk walk. At times, images of Claire's injury swam before her eyes and she broke into a jog for a few hundred feet. She was grateful the road was mostly downhill.

The night creeped by, and she had plenty of time to think about how unfair she'd been to Claire over the past few days. What had happened to Sena's mom wasn't Claire's fault; it wasn't Sena's fault. Songyee had made a lifetime of decisions that had led her to that point.

Sena sorrowed for the mother she'd never really known. The mother that had chosen drug abuse over her daughter time after time.

Walking through the night, thirsty and cold, she had a sudden flash of insight. She remembered her thirst on the life raft. She would have done anything for water then; she even drank seawater she knew might kill her.

She had known what it was like to need something so badly you'd sacrifice your own life to have it. With this new perspective, she could kind of understand her mom. It didn't justify what Songyee had done, though it explained a little.

A bubbling stream of mountain water cascaded over the rocks on one side of the road. Sena stopped to let the cold water wash away the blood on her hands. Then she brought handfuls of it to her lips and drank the unbelievably icy, pure liquid.

Water was a luxury she never took for granted now.

Refreshed, she hurried her pace. It felt like she'd been traveling for miles. Was there anyone on this mountain besides her? Was she a fool for going off on her own? What if she didn't find anyone? Or worse, what if she did find someone and they wouldn't help? Or wanted to hurt her?

Questions swirled in her mind, and the moon sank behind Sena until her moon shadow stretched long in front of her.

True darkness was coming to the mountain.

Hours later, Sena could barely put one foot in front of the other. She was so cold and tired, and pain was splitting her head. It was late September, with nighttime temperatures nearing 40 degrees Fahrenheit. She brought her arms inside her sleeves and wrapped them around her, next to her skin, trying to get warm.

It was so dark she could barely see to stay on the road, and she shuffled along. One thing had changed, for which she was grateful: her paralyzing fear of the dark was gone. She knew now that she would walk through a thousand nights for Claire if it would save her.

She continued down the road, stumbling occasionally, and praying for a miracle. She had never prayed so much in her life, not even on the lifeboat.

She realized that she had much more to lose now. Like

Kade had said, Claire and Ted were like parents to her, and even Kade himself was becoming a friend.

Though the temperature was still dropping, Sena looked around and thought it looked a little lighter. Trees and rocks glowed faintly, though she couldn't see anything clearly.

The sun would be up soon. The thought gave her little hope. She had almost reached the end of her endurance, and she hadn't seen a single person.

As the first rays of sun broke over the mountains, cutting through the darkness, it was as if a weight was lifted from her. The density of night was dispelled, and in the brilliant sunlight, she was awed by the beauty and majesty surrounding her.

She stumbled along the edge of the road. She saw forests of old trees carpeted with moss and mushrooms, and then a meadow of wildflowers, not yet touched by frost. There she made the best find yet, a clump of flaming red bushes blanketed with purple berries.

Sena left the road and gingerly picked a berry with her ruined hands, then popped it in her mouth and chewed cautiously. The tender skin split between her teeth and her mouth filled with the taste of a blueberry gone mad. It was like eating pure, sweet wildness.

She took a few more berries and ate them while she walked. She decided she'd never tasted anything as delicious as the mountain berries and wished she knew what they were. The sun continued to light the sky, and she picked up her pace.

Less than an hour later, the morning breeze brought a welcome sound to her ears. An engine. She turned to look behind her, and discovered the sound was ahead of her. It must be a car coming up the mountain.

The sound didn't get any closer, so she kept walking, trying to figure out what it was. A second engine roared to life, and with horror, she realized what she was hearing. *Motorcycles.*

It must be the motorcycle gang from the previous day. They'd probably passed the site of the wreck without noticing it, and spent the night here camping. Now they were getting ready to leave.

They would be going the wrong way though.

Sena knew they might be the only other people on the mountain and she was going to miss them.

She began to run.

Each time she heard another engine start, she was spurred to greater speed until she was racing down the highway. Too soon, she heard a mighty roar as they rode out together.

Wait! she wanted to scream at them, her lungs on fire. Her headache was worse now, and she had blisters on her feet from walking through the night. She had a stitch in her side and she was nauseous, but she put aside all of those feelings and ran to save Claire.

Claire, the only woman who had ever really wanted to be a mother to her.

She mouthed Claire's name to the beat of her hiking boots pounding down the road.

Claire. Claire. Claire.

Then the chant changed to a prayer: *Please. Please. Please.*

Sena rounded a bend in the road and saw a sign for a campground and ranger station up ahead. The last motorcycle was pulling out from the access road. She waved, but he was already turning.

His back tire kicked up rocks as he gunned his engine

and rode away.

Sena staggered to a stop in the middle of the road with a sob. She tried to shout to the rider, but she couldn't catch her breath. The air was too thin here. She gasped and struggled as her lightheadedness drove her to her knees, and then to the ground.

Sena passed out. A small, crumpled form in the middle of the empty highway.

CHAPTER TWENTY-TWO

WHEN SENA AWOKE, SHE was on a cot in a small cabin. A woman stood with her back to Sena, talking to someone. When she turned, Sena recognized the biker mom from the day before when they'd siphoned gas at the jet skis. Her daughter, Sassy, was at the table too, eating a bowl of oatmeal.

"Hi, Sena," she said.

When Sena tried to sit up, the woman shook her head. "Stay still," she said. "Doc's gonna be here in a minute to sew up that split in your scalp and the cuts on your hands."

"You've got a doctor?" Sena asked, sitting up anyway. "My family needs help. Our car went off the road up the mountain and—"

"I know," said the woman. "A couple of us remembered you from yesterday. Figured we'd better check your back trail and see if there were any other survivors."

"I need to get back there and help," said Sena. "Is there any way you can give me a ride back up?"

"I don't think so. You've got altitude sickness and a concussion, and I wouldn't be surprised if you're hypothermic and dehydrated too. No, you're staying right here."

"But I have to know…" Sena was suddenly afraid to

know. What if she'd taken too long? What if it was too late?

"About your family?" the woman finished. "Don't worry, honey. You saved them." She held up a walkie-talkie. "The gang already found them and got them out of your truck. They're all still alive, and they're almost up to the road and the bikes. They'll be loading them up and bringing them down here soon."

She looked at Sena carefully. "Your mom's in bad shape. You know that though, don't you?"

Sena didn't correct her when she called Claire her mom. She liked how it sounded.

"How did you know I was there? I didn't think anyone saw me. You all rode away."

"*Almost* all rode away," said the woman, with a pointed look at Sassy. "Do you remember that book you gave my daughter?"

"I was reading it in bed last night and it fell behind the bed," Sassy piped up. "Mama was mad."

"Yep, we had to stay behind and look for that blasted book. I came out of the cabin just in time to see you fall. After I saw you were in trouble, I got on the radio and told everyone what was going on. They all remembered you and your dad from yesterday. Most people would just as soon shoot you as look at you these days, but we could tell you folks were different. We wanted to help.

"We've got one guy who used to be a paramedic. We call him Doc. He's going to patch you all up and then you can recover here a while. This cabin is normally a gift shop. There are a few beds in the back where you can stay while you rest up."

Sena blinked rapidly, tears of relief and gratitude ready to spill. "You've been so nice, and I don't even know your name."

"Before I joined the gang I was Maria Angeles," said the woman. "Everyone calls me Angel now."

Sena smiled. Of course she'd been saved by an Angel.

Angel was as good as her word. Within the hour, Sena's family (she couldn't think of a better word for them) was brought to the ranger station and Doc did what he could for them.

Though Sena's injuries were easily treated, the cuts on her hands remained painful and stiff for a long time. Kade put antibiotic ointment on them for her, and helped with as much of the work as he could, though his foot kept him from getting around very well. He had a sprain and possibly some crushed bones in his ankle. Without an X-ray, Doc said he couldn't be sure how bad it was, so Kade was to stay off the foot as much as possible.

Ted and Claire's injuries were more serious and they were confined to bed for a few weeks. Ted had a concussion and an extremely painful fractured sternum. There wasn't any treatment for it besides bed rest and time.

He didn't complain, though his injuries probably were the most painful of all of them. They all agreed that he should get the lion's share of the ibuprofen Sena had taken from the Clarks' medicine cabinet.

Doc said Kade had done exactly the right thing by stopping Claire's blood loss and keeping her warm through that first long night. After Doc cleaned and sewed up her wound, he told them all how lucky they were she was still alive. When he said she was a fighter, Claire looked straight at Sena and said she had a lot worth fighting for.

Sena didn't answer. Instead, she reached for Claire's hand and gave it a squeeze.

The gruff EMP cautioned them about keeping Claire's wound clean and watching for infection. Sena hurried to the bag of medications and pulled out a bottle Jodie was supposed to take for a UTI which had cleared up on its own.

"Will this work?" she asked Doc, handing him the bottle. His craggy face brightened when he read the name. "Cipro. Yes, this is perfect." He looked inside and counted the capsules. "There's even a full dose here. If you didn't save her life with your midnight hike, you just saved it now."

Sena was a minor celebrity. Sassy came up with the nickname 'Nightwalker' for her. She'd covered seven miles in the dark, not including the steep climb from the wreck to the road.

Not only that, but she'd discovered the only patch of huckleberries still on the bush this late in the season. After Angel had seen the telltale stains on Sena's hands, she'd taken Sassy berry picking and they brought back a big bucket of the fresh fruit.

Angel made the berries into huckleberry crisp in an old Dutch oven they found in the rangers' supplies. Even though she cooked a lot, there was barely enough to go around.

Kade had a bite on his fork and was raising it to his mouth when they heard Ted shout. "Kade! Stop right there!"

Kade's fork froze in midair.

From the bed, Ted said more calmly, "I believe you owe me that dessert."

Sena giggled, while Kade groaned and put the fork down. "You know I can outrun you, right?" But he surrendered the treat good-naturedly.

The bikers had offered to bring the group's bicycles and supplies up from the wreckage for a share of the food. Ted and Claire quickly agreed, and by the time the bikers left for good, they were settled into the cabin with enough food and supplies for several months.

Before they left, Angel offered to come back and check on the family in the spring. Ted said, "Come see us in Lookout Falls. We'll be at Milt Kerns' farm."

Sena heard this news with surprise. She'd thought they would have to spend the winter in the ranger cabin.

"We're leaving?" she asked.

Ted nodded. "Although it seems like we have a lot of food now, it's not enough to get us through the winter. As soon as we're feeling a bit better, we're going to push on."

"Don't stay too long then," advised Angel. "They close this road every winter for a reason. I wish we could tell your family you're here, but we're turning south. We've got people here anxious to get home."

"We understand, Angel," said Claire. "You've already done far more for us than we can ever thank you for."

"God bless you, and we'll see you next spring."

The family waved goodbye to the gang, and began the slow, tedious process of recovery.

On the morning they were to leave, Sena stood outside the door of the cabin and looked out over the majesty of the mountains. It was hard to believe they were finally leaving. They were still a little tender, but everyone was anxious to get back on the road. Ted explained that if they took it carefully and didn't exert themselves, they'd be okay.

He and Kade joked around while they loaded the bicycles with the special saddlebags Kade had been working on. It still amazed Sena to see them getting along. Kade had changed a lot in the past few months. She knew he still mourned for Charity, but he'd matured, and he was over his bitter anger at her loss.

Lately he'd started teasing Sena and flirting gently with her. She wasn't sure she wanted it to go anywhere. Now and then she thought about their almost-kiss on the cruise ship and decided to wait and see what happened.

Claire came out of the cabin and closed the door firmly behind her. She put an arm around Sena, and the two stood in companionable silence enjoying the mountain morning.

"What are you thinking about?" Claire asked after a long, peaceful moment.

"Oh, nothing. Just the trip. Are you going to be up to it? Do you think it's too soon?"

"I'm more worried that it's too late. Hopefully the weather will hold."

There was silence again, and then Claire said, "I remember you said once you might not fit in with our family, or that Dee might not like you. Are you still worried about that?"

Sena thought about it before answering. Finally she said, "Not anymore. I mean, it might be kind of weird at first, but we'll figure it out."

Claire pulled her closer in a one-armed hug. "That's exactly right. We're family now, and that means we stick together."

Ted got on his bike, and motioned for them to join

him.

"Come on, Sena," said Claire, taking her hand. "It's time to go home."

CHAPTER TWENTY-THREE

EPILOGUE

DEE SAT IN front of the fire in her grandpa's house, watching Angela, a neighbor and close family friend, fill the Christmas stockings. Unlike Dee's previous Christmases, the stockings weren't stuffed to overflowing, and the pile of presents under the tree was small, but it was going to be a wonderful morning, maybe her best Christmas ever.

Dee looked around the room and felt so blessed. Her grandpa sat in his chair, tapping his crystal ball cane on his leg and humming along with Angela's teenage son Hyrum as he played, "Silent Night," on the guitar. Her boyfriend Mason sang the bass line, and Angela joined in with the alto. Dee looked into each face, knowing they were lucky to be together.

She wished her parents were here to enjoy the peace and safety she and the others had fought so hard to protect.

They finished the song and Mason suggested, "How about some Jingle Bells?"

"How about something less likely to wake the kids up?" Angela countered.

Mason's little brother Sammy had been in and out of his room all night, coming downstairs to remind them

Ellisa Barr

not to eat the cookies they'd left out for Santa, and asking, yet again, whether Santa could fit down the pipe of the wood burning stove.

Hyrum began to sing a Christmas song Dee didn't recognize. It had simple lyrics about Santa and toys and children. Hyrum's voice soared on the chorus, and she closed her eyes like the words suggested, listening to the skies, hoping, for one fanciful moment, she'd hear Kris Kringle and the jingle bell.

Instead, she heard... voices. Outside. *Wait. Voices outside?*

Dee's eyes snapped open and she saw the dog jump to his feet and trot to the door.

"Want me to get the shotgun?" she asked Grandpa in a low voice.

Grandpa shook his head. "I don't think so. Look at Jasper."

Jasper stood at the door, ears pricked and tail wagging broadly. His mouth was open in a wide doggy grin.

"Take the lantern and see who it is, Maddie. I reckon whoever's out there is chilled to the bone."

Dee stood and nudged Jasper out of the way so she could open the door. It was dark outside, and the warm glow of the lantern illuminated the front porch.

"Hello?" called Dee.

"Dee?" came a voice from the yard. "Is that you?"

Dee's heart began to pound and tears formed instantly in her eyes. She'd waited so long to hear that voice.

"Mom?" she said, already halfway down the stairs.

Dee found herself sandwiched between her mom and her dad. They were all laughing and crying at the same time, while Jasper ran around them in circles, barking.

Grandpa stood in the doorway, holding up the lantern

208

Dee had set down. "Is that my girl?" he asked.

"Dad! You're okay!" Claire hurried up the stairs to her father, and Dee noticed how her own dad and another young man supported her. They were so thin it made Dee's heart ache.

There was still one more person in the yard. A small Asian girl with glasses and long black braids stood uncertainly at the edge of the light.

"Come on in," invited Dee.

"Are you sure? I won't be intruding?"

Dee's heart warmed to the girl and she studied her for a moment. "We're going to be friends, I think, aren't we? I've really needed a friend."

She reached out a hand to the girl and brought her into the circle of light.

Thank you for reading *Voyage*!
I hope you enjoyed it and will consider recommending it
to your friends.

Book 3 of the *Powerless Nation* Series, coming
Winter 2015

Sign up to be notified of new releases at:
www.ellisabarr.com/newbooks

About the Author

Ellisa grew up in a small town in Idaho, even smaller than the fictitious town of Lookout Falls. In the summer, almost entirely cut off from friends and other entertainment, she became a voracious reader. When she misbehaved as a tween, her parents despaired of finding a suitable punishment, because the only thing she wanted to do was read. Finally they resorted to grounding her from books. Her friends thought she had the best parents ever. Ellisa agrees.

She lives with her husband, two kids, a dog and a cat in southern California, where she thinks she should do more to be ready for earthquakes. She teaches music and homeschools her children in the winter, and in the summer she hides out from the heat with a stack of books.

Website: www.ellisabarr.com
Facebook: www.facebook.com/ellisabarrbooks

Made in the USA
San Bernardino, CA
05 January 2015